I0586248

Fiery Arrow

Sheila R. Lamb

Triple Fire Press

Fiery Arrow

Triple Fire Press

Copyright © 2022 by Sheila R. Lamb

Cover design copyright © 2022 Amy Chae Design

Second edition

First edition published by Solstice Publishing, 2014

ISBN 978-0-9838552-7-9

The characters and events portrayed in this book are fictitious or used fictitiously. Any similarity to real persons, living or dead, is purely coincidental and not intended by the author.

All rights reserved. No part of this publication may be reproduced, distributed, or transmitted in any form or by any means, including photocopying, recording, or other electronic or mechanical methods, without the prior written permission of the publisher, except in the case of brief quotations embodied in critical reviews and certain other noncommercial uses permitted by copyright law. For permission requests, contact Triple Fire Press.

"Between St. Patrick and St. Brigid, the columns of the Irish, there was so great a friendship of charity that they had but one heart and one mind..."

Book of Armagh, 8th Century

CHAPTER 1

Brigid

F otharit, Leinster, Éire, 5th Century:
   I crept around the corner and leaned against the rough thatch wall. Damp mists disguised any shadow I might have cast as I hid in the crevice created by the opened oak door and outer wall of our house. Maithghean, the chief druid, and my father, Dubhtach, a druid seer, spoke in hushed tones. Their conversation was about me. I willed the sounds of the bawling cows and snuffling pigs from our farm into the background.

"Dubhtach, Brigid knows who she is and she's keeping it from us."

"How can you be so sure? I'm her father."

"And you are biased, blinded by your relationship." Maithghean pounded his fist on the table . "I knew of her powers before she was born. I knew-"

Father cut him off. "You know nothing! Her mother lived with you for a short time but you hold no prophecy over my daughter!"

Fear rose within me. I had glimmers, faulty strains of memory, which gave me a vague awareness of before. My past was like a scattered puzzle. How could Maithghean know what I had been, when I struggled to grasp one tangible piece?

"We must test her, Dubhtach." His voice dropped to a low whisper, ignoring my father's reference to their long history together. "If she deceived us about her powers and knowledge of her former life, we must bring her to the sacred circle."

"The circle? No. That's too extreme." Father paced. His footsteps fell heavy on the earthen floor.

"She can be tested in the oak grove!" Maithghean's voice rose as if my father hadn't spoken. "We have to discover her powers. She's druid-born!"

"This idea is ridiculous!" I was glad my father came to my defense. "It wouldn't work. I taught Brigid myself. She *is* druid-born and trained and she would pass any test you gave."

"Any test?" Maithghean hissed. "She couldn't fool us under the Test of the Ancients."

A shiver went down my spine. Scared children whispered superstitions about the Test of the Ancients. Parents threatened them with dreams of the Ancient ghosts, forever watching. The druids secretly conjured the spirits of the Ancients, the Original inhabitants of Éire. I had never seen the rite performed.

Father stood firm. "Absolutely not. To put a young woman through that ritual is certain death."

Maithghean shrugged. I heard the casual drop of his robes, as if he didn't care whether I lived or died. "It's only 'certain death' if she is not one of them. The Ancients protect their own. Brigid won't be at risk."

Father didn't answer and the silence lengthened.

What if only dreams haunted my sleep? Dreams and nothing more? Yet even I knew my dreams were unexplainable. The visions I had of the Old Ones were unmentionable because Maithghean wanted to pry their meaning from me. He searched for answers I didn't understand.

I remained outside, crouched behind the door, with my hands and knees in the mud. I waited for my father to answer Maithghean's claim. Nothing. The two men left the house.

I stayed behind the door until I was certain they wouldn't return. I was shocked that my father would allow me to undergo the sacred – and dangerous – test. My palms, damp and brown with the mud that stuck to them, betrayed my fear. I wiped them on my skirt, and hoped the tell tale signs would blend in with the green and brown woven plaid.

"Be careful, Brigid."

I jumped as my mother spoke. She had witnessed my eavesdropping as she walked from the stable. Her gray cloak, evidence of her slave status, blended in with the sky behind her but her brown eyes burned through me.

"Mother-" I hoped she wouldn't tell Father about my spying. She cut off my words, angrily meeting me in three quick strides.

"Don't allow them to catch you! Maithghean can punish you in any way he sees fit." Her intensity caught me off guard. Maithghean. Our chief druid. He wielded more power than our chieftain. Rarely was my mother harsh with me. Then she pointed west. Father and Maithghean walked along the path, the side of our house clearly visible. They could have seen me.

"I won't get caught. Please don't tell Father that I was listening."

She pulled me by the arm and led me to the darkened stable. "What did you hear?"

I hesitated, unsure if I should tell her about the Test of the Ancients. Yet already my life was at risk and Mother had studied druid lore in her own country.

"They want me for the sacred test, Mother. The Test of the Ancients. Maithghean believes he can-" I stopped. "He believes he can find out things... about me," I finished lamely.

"You're different, Brigid. You always have been, from the moment of your conception. Maithghean knew this before you were born."

"How can Maithghean know there is something about me...something I don't even know?"

"Think about it Brigid. You have always shown signs of having special powers."

"What kind of powers?" I asked, although I already knew the answer. They were the things I kept hidden.

"As a child, you could draw light to you. Passers-by claimed they knew when I left you alone. They saw a fiery glow through our doorway."

I thought of the heat that gathered around my brow when my anger grew.

"Peasant talk, really. But there is some truth to it. Do you remember, Brigid?"

"No." I pulled the hood of my cloak closer. "That doesn't answer Maithghean's suspicions of me. And why disturb the Ancients?"

"Because others are jealous of your natural powers," Mother's gaze caused another shiver to engulf me. "What you were born with, others have sought their whole lives to attain, with blood and sweat and hard work. You come by these gifts naturally. They will hate you for it."

A cold hand snaked around my throat. I gasped, unable to speak. My heart pounded. I kicked and thrashed but a hand held me down. If I lay still, I could breathe. In the dark, shapes and shadows were visible but nothing else.

A sticky, sweet substance was forced into my mouth, causing me to gag. I coughed and choked, but the tingling began immediately. The shadows pulled my nightclothes over my head. I tried to raise my arm to fight, but my limbs were heavy, weighted.

They carried me outside, naked, lifted high above their heads, a dozen hands supporting me. The dark sky wavered like the sea. The moon remained dark, hidden in the final phases of her cycle. Waves of nausea passed over me, and I swallowed hard against the stickiness at the back of my mouth. I wanted to cry out but I couldn't make a sound.

The shadows placed me on a wooden surface, a motion that caused the world to spin. Tiny bonfires blurred together in a single circle of light which surrounded me. I couldn't stop the vertigo, nor could I grasp the wood beneath me. The sickening feeling overwhelmed me.

The shadows stepped back and left me exposed in the circle's center. Tremors convulsed through my body, and I flailed uncontrollably. The weight pressed against me until I could deny it no longer.

The shadows watched.

Flashes of memory revealed themselves to me. I saw the man who appeared in my dreams. Who was he? Where was he? Others then, the Ancients, Lugh and Fodla, Macha and Dagda. Images flew by in my mind's eye.

A low voice snarled in my ear. "Who do you see?"

Danger. I searched for some way to ground, to connect with the earth so I wouldn't be lost in this otherworldly realm.

I saw a flash of the man's face again. An incomprehensible series of jumbled images filled my mind. I knew him. I hadn't met him but I knew him. *Patricius,* in the Roman tongue. *Patrick, Padraic...*

"Help me."

"Who? Who will help you?" Warm breath rested on my throat. The voice couldn't be trusted.

My mind split in confusion, pulled between the present and the past. I viewed the images from a distance and tried to make sense of the random pieces, looking for the thread that tied them together. Patrick was the common theme that appeared before me. I could observe him from my induced state...no, more than that. I knew him. I heard him, his thoughts. And then, I saw my life unfold beside his, my childhood up to this point...and within this, I saw myself with him in a time before... him but not him...*Patrick, Padraic.*

I found I could watch the scenes play out, my childhood here and my past beyond, until another rude awakening from the distrusted voice jolted me back.

"Brigid, tell me. Who are you?"

A voice deep within me spoke. My own voice – yet not my own. *Don't tell Maithghean. Protect Patrick. Protect yourself.*

CHAPTER 2

Patrick

Bannaven Taberniae, Britannia, 5th Century:

"Your roll." Patrick grinned at his friend and tossed the pair of dice across the oak-hewn dining table.

"What should I wager?" Linus leaned back on his couch, rattling the dice in his hand with a self-assured smirk. "Another denarii?" He threw the game pieces. Doubles.

Patrick laughed in spite of himself. "You've won again." He drained his silver mug of ale.

"When are you going to pay me the denarii you owe?" Linus asked good-naturedly. They both knew the debt that had accumulated throughout their training years would remain unpaid.

Darys, the ten-year-old Pictish houseboy, appeared with another tray of beer. His eyes were puffy from lack of sleep, and he wobbled slightly as he set two more cups before his master.

"Are we keeping you up too late?" Patrick asked. "Well, this will be our last game and last ale."

Linus yawned. "It will? I thought I was staying here until your parents returned from casting their vote." The dice clinked in his cupped hand, assuring him of another win.

"We can play until sunrise, but let the boy sleep. Go on." Patrick motioned for the servant to be on his way. "Good thing we don't have training tomorrow. I'd never be able to lift a sword, drinking at this rate."

Linus snorted. They practiced drills reserved for wealthy sons of Roman citizens. In their last year, the young men knew they received only perfunctory training of basic battlefield techniques, weaponry, and ceremonial duties. They would follow their father's careers after their army service; their futures clearly and definitively planned.

Suddenly, a sharp crack reverberated through the house. Patrick gripped the table and Darys threw himself onto silk cushions piled on the floor.

"Raiders!" Linus sat still in his chair, as if frozen.

"Here? We're miles up the river. Raiders never sail this far inland," Patrick whispered.

Another ripping crash ricocheted off the cool plaster walls, and the sound of splitting oak told him the solid door that protected his family's home stood no longer.

Patrick peeked cautiously out the dining room entrance. "I'm going to get my sword. It's in my bedchamber."

"No, Patrick. It's too dangerous. Don't go out there!" Linus hadn't moved from his chair and Darys cowered beneath the cushions.

"What else are we going to do? Do you have your sword with you?"

Linus reached into the tall leather of his boot. "Only a dagger."

"It's better than nothing. Stay here with Darys until I return."

Patrick darted out into the atrium as the sounds of breaking glassware and ceramics echoed throughout the villa. He ran into his room and searched for his sword at his bedside—not there. His head spun. There it lay, in a slim shaft of moonlight, left carelessly atop his trunk. He cursed himself for leaving it out of its usual place and blamed Linus for the distraction of dice and ale.

From the far end of the garden, servants screamed for help in their native tongue, rather than the Latin his father required them to speak. Close by, on the other side of the wall, a woman cried out, a wrenching sound that made his heart stop. Cold sweat lined his brow. These raiders would come for him and kill him. The thud of footsteps approached his doorway.

Deo juvante. With God's help, Patrick prayed, something he didn't often do. He wrapped his long fingers around the familiar hilt of his sword. From his requisite training, he knew his sword thrusts were as accurate as his arrow marks, but he hadn't been tested in battle. He tightened his grip with a nervous breath and raised the weapon.

Four muscular men with long, unkempt mustaches burst through the door. Before he could swing the sword with a cutting slice as he had practiced, the intruders lunged for him. His head exploded in pain as it slammed onto the floor. Hard, callused hands grabbed at his arms and legs. He pushed against the huge men covered in dirty plaid cloaks, anything to get away from them. With his free hand, he waved his sword, struggling for an angle. Several hard blows to his stomach took the wind from him and forced him to drop the heavy sword. The iron clattered loudly on the tiled floor.

Patrick's fear gave way to fury, and he bit his attacker's arm, tasting the old salt of sweat and seawater. He kicked and yelled and his legs thrashed wildly against the intruders who held him down. Their long matted hair covered his face and he bit at that as well. Stringy strands and disgusting grit filled his mouth. His knee struck one man's groin, but the raider merely grunted. The intruders seemed to be made of solid rock. Outnumbered, he wished his legion were here—wait, where was Linus?

Two men held him fast to the floor while the others bound his hands. They weren't trying to kill him; they would have done it by now. Ropes, tight and cutting, secured his wrists behind his back as he lay panting, face down in his bedroom doorway. A man in leather breeches, issued from the Roman army and similar to his own, ran past.

"Linus!" he cried, but his friend had gone. Where were the guards? Linus would call them.

He faintly recognized the kidnappers' Irish Gaelic, a distant cousin of the local Welsh dialect, before a sack went over his head. Rough, woven flax scratched his face, and it smelled like the inside of a stable, dank and musty.

Forceful hands carried Patrick outside and a gravelly voice shouted orders in Irish. Clanking metal told him these thieves took his family's heirlooms, lost forever. Cold night air slapped his body as his captor hefted him over his shoulder and took him from the only home he had ever known. Punches and blade-thrusts between servants and sailors accosted his ears. He bucked in an effort to remove the sack, kicking at his captor with his long legs. Suddenly, the raider grunted and stumbled, throwing Patrick hard to the ground.

Still hooded and bound, Patrick hoped not to be trampled in the melee as he twisted his bound body in an effort to stand. The clash of swords and daggers rang in his ears, and the smell of smoke burned his nostrils. Another pair of hands surprised him and dragged him across the cool grass.

"I got him good, didn't I? A nice stab to the shoulder made him drop you quickly."

Patrick gratefully gulped in cool air, tinged with smoke, as Siculus, his father's manservant, pulled the stifling sack from his head.

Who were these beasts tearing apart his home? Where were the guards? Linus should have summoned them by now. His eyes adjusted to the darkness punctuated by the flames of the burning house.

A grove of oaks partially hid them. Patrick craned his neck, trying to see the villa, while Siculus struggled to untie the ropes from Patrick's hands and feet.

"Head down!" Siculus fumbled with the cords on Patrick's wrists. Between the haze of billowing smoke and the scramble of terrified servants, Patrick couldn't see what happened to his home.

"Hurry," Patrick urged. Although they had refuge in the oak grove, it wouldn't be for long.

"I dropped my blade when I stabbed that large brute. I have no knife to cut the ropes," Siculus said.

Patrick squinted through the darkness again. Still no sign of the Roman guards. Perhaps they could hide amongst the oaks until the sacking ended. His shoulders ached and his hands, gone numb, hung loose around the small of his back. Siculus tugged and pulled on the tight ropes, making only limited progress, when his fumbling fingers stopped their movement.

Dampness spattered Patrick's cheek, and the strong coppery scent of blood assaulted his senses. Siculus gasped, then gurgled, and fell with a quiet slump into the soft earth.

Patrick found himself tossed over the raider's shoulder once again like a sack of grain. Blood rushed to his head as he thrashed in an effort to escape, and he gasped when they turned. Siculus lay face down with his own dagger next to his throat. Blood drained in pools around him. Patrick's stomach churned and bile rose bitter into his mouth. His minor skirmishes hadn't prepared him for the sight of death. Not of one so close.

Patrick struggled against the raider as the man reached down to pick up the fallen blade next to Siculus. From his upside down vantage, Patrick recognized the well-trodden path that led to the river. His captor slid along the muddied trail to boats that bumped gently against each other at the curve in the river's bend. Patrick lifted his aching head from his captor's broad back and saw his home engulfed in flames.

Patrick sat, wedged between sacks of oats from his own cellar, with two of his houseboys, including Darys. The raiders had removed the ropes from his wrists and replaced them with chains, joining three captives together by neck and wrist. The ache between Patrick's shoulder blades ceased as he could now change position and, as long as Darys did the same, rested his hands on his knees.

Darys looked thin and scared. Patrick squirmed with a stab of guilt about keeping the boy up all night serving ale. The youngster glanced up at him as if searching for a hopeful solution. Seeing that his master had none, he turned away. Darys's fate is the same, Patrick thought. A lifetime of servitude merely changed locations.

The sailors pushed off westward from the river's mouth toward the wide sea as the sun began to rise. The pirate surveyed the fleet of four boats, his crew, and its booty, Patrick noted, with apparent approval. He must be the captain. Only a trace of blood marked where Siculus had stabbed his shoulder.

Patrick's father, Calpornius, had told him stories about the rough, barrel-chested men from across the Irish Sea who stealthily approached British villages in the dark of night. They tied their rowboats - no, *currachs*, his father had told him once. The Irish word sounded like a cough - to trees along the river's edge, stealthily, in the darkness. They'd never show their face in the sunlight, his father had said. The causes of the Irish raids were simple: starvation and isolation. They needed slaves, goods, and new bloodlines on their barbarian island.

Patrick forced his thoughts away from the idea of slavery and focused on the boat as daylight beckoned. The oval-shaped craft had tapered ends allowing it to skim unnoticed into the mouth of the Sabrina River. The men sliced their oars toward the cold, choppy waters of the Irish Sea, and he wondered how the simple watercraft would fare.

Patrick watched the captain while he rowed.

"Seamus!" A sailor called from another boat, and the pirate turned his head. His name is Seamus. Patrick didn't know if the information would do him any good, but it gave him something else to think about besides servitude.

The men spoke across the water to each other in their native Irish and Patrick listened carefully. The language ought to have been unfamiliar, but as the raiders issued their commands, he found he understood their words.

Confused, he closed his eyes and searched through his memories of tutoring sessions. Welsh, his native language, and Latin were both spoken in his home. Occasionally, Dyfed, his tutor, taught him words from the Greeks. But Irish? How did he know this barbaric language? A queasy feeling, beyond seasickness, churned in his stomach.

"Fergus, we've got several men who will make good workers, laborers on farms. Or, we may trade a few." Seamus called to his rowing partner over the splash of oars hitting the waves.

"Aye, then. Will the young women work as well?" Fergus flashed a knowing grin at his captain.

"Perhaps," Seamus answered. "They'd make good wives for some of you men."

"The last thing I need is another wife!" Fergus ribbed in reply. "Maybe I'll sire a few children with them instead." The men guffawed.

They rowed in unison, while Patrick cradled his head in his arms, listening.

"The boy, though..." Seamus said. "That lad put up a good fight." Patrick glanced up at the huge man and saw him rub his tongue on the inside of his cheek. Patrick recalled, with satisfaction, one swift blow he had landed during his struggle.

Fergus shrugged. "You could use him on your own land in Antrim, Seamus. Your flocks are growing and you're going to need help with the plowing and planting."

Seamus's muscles rippled through his shoulders and chest as he rowed, shirtless. Patrick trembled at the thought of working for him...and he trembled even more as his mind continued to process with ease the pirate's conversation.

"The boy is tall. He looks to be in good health; he could manage the sheep on the hills. I'll keep him for myself. Maybe a few of these young girls as well, if we get enough trade at the harbor."

CHAPTER 3

Brigid

As a small child, I believed people looked upon me with envy because my father was a druid, a seer who read signs and prophecies. He even arranged for me to learn plant lore from our healer for a few afternoons to gauge my interest. This increased my childish pride, my surety that I was special as a druid's daughter and I skipped through the fort every day, head held high. Then, one day, I discovered I had been wrong.

A woman approached me as I sat outside the granary, collecting rocks, while Mother pounded grain in the quern, "Hello, Brigid." The woman's words were kind but her tone was sharp. "My name is Sena."

A boy shuffled behind her. He had dirt on their cheeks, and his wool leggings were torn.

Sena wore gold ornaments in her hair and bangles of gold on her wrists. I had never seen a woman so decorated with jewelry at the granary. I glanced toward my mother inside, in her plain gray cloak, intent on her work.

"You are such a pretty little girl," Sena said. "You could have been my daughter. How old are you now? Five? Six?" She ran her thin finger over the gold-knotted brooch that pinned my cloak together, the only bit of jewelry I possessed. "Meet your brother, Bacene."

I was puzzled by the woman's words. The dirty little boy she pulled to her side wasn't my brother. I had no siblings. Bacene and I stared at each other. I had seen him before, running wild with his older brothers, while his mother bartered for goods at the market.

"Mother!" I called. She looked up from the pestle and she saw Sena near me.

"Stay away from my daughter." Mother said to Sena, her voice low and dangerous.

"You're nothing but a servant. A Pict, a slave brought here over the water," Sena sneered. My mother's tone had no effect on her. "This girl needs to know her family!"

Mother came to my side and gripped my hand. "Come now, Brigid." She was quiet but stern. I knew when to obey her. But I noticed for the first time that she had an accent different from Sena's and mine.

I followed mother inside the granary and began to sack the flour she'd ground from the grain.

"I'm sure you have plenty of work to do, slaving away on the farm," Sena said from the doorway.

Mother's face burned bright while we worked under Sena's mocking gaze.

"What's a Pict?" I asked as we walked home, pushing the cart that held our bag of flour.

"They're my people," Mother answered. "They're far away, over the sea, near Britannia."

"Where's Britannia? Who was that woman? Why was she so mean?" All my questions were met with furious silence. I wanted to know more about the Picts and people across the sea, far away from Éire.

"Brigid," she said hoarsely. "Go feed the animals. I'll be out to milk the cows soon." She turned away from me, strode into the house, and slammed the door. I had never seen her this livid.

I went to the stable. I had never fed the animals by myself before. My mother had always supervised. The bin by the wall was full of fresh oats for the horses, a task I wouldn't have been able to complete if it were less than full. It would have been impossible for me to reach the oats. The horses waited and watched me scoop oats into the wooden pail. With both hands, I dragged the pail to the horses' trough, struggling to lift it. It was heavier than I imagined but finally succeeded. I grabbed armfuls of hay for the cows, one after the other, until their cribs overflowed. They needed to be milked but I couldn't reach the stool and the pail Mother used.

Last, were the pigs. I didn't like feeding those animals in their muddy pen and preferred the coziness inside the stables. Mother always kept a pail behind the house full of slops, and I trudged back to get it.

I heard voices as I approached our house. Father. He must have returned from the oak grove.

"Brocca, I'm sorry she approached you in such a manner, but I can't control what she says."

"Why, Dubhtach? Why after all these years? I thought she accepted the way things are now!" Mother's voice quivered. I didn't understand how that boy Bacene could be my brother. Worst of all, I didn't know why Sena's harshness made my mother cry.

I waited outside, unsure of what to do. If I moved the slop pail, it would make a noise and they would hear me. They would probably stop the conversation if they knew I was there and I would never be able to find out what was happening. I crouched against the thatched wall.

"You know Sena refuses to divorce. She refuses to allow a second wife. She refuses to agree to any compromises set by the Brehons."

"And you have used that as an excuse for not marrying me at Beltane," Mother hissed. "Is that how it will always be Dubhtach, relying on Sena's irrational feelings?"

"You know why we can't marry," he said, his voice low.

"Because you, and everyone here, consider me your servant. Why don't you sell me at your whim?"

My stomach twisted. My parents weren't married? Mother was his servant? I was raised in relative wealth due to Father's standing in the druid order; he was part of a privileged class. Our home was large and airy, colorfully decorated with the wools and plaids Mother wove. Our tables and benches were good solid oak. Not only did we live off our dairy farming, but Father received the druid's portions donated by all in our village each year.

I had seen slaves in other households, like when we visited Maithghean. Non-free persons, usually prisoners of war or sometimes a raid, were a part of life. They had no freedom to leave as they pleased. Slaves were tolerated with politeness, but most of the higher classes, especially the druids and brehons, didn't go out of their way to talk to them. I wasn't allowed to play with their children.

"You know I love you, Brocca; that has never changed." He used his soothing voice to Mother, the same calm tone he used when he issued dire predictions from the throwing sticks.

She laughed. "You have everything you desire, Dubhtach. Sena can raise your sons, while I raise your daughter and wait on you from dawn till dusk. And you know perfectly well that neither Sena or I would tolerate each other to run a household together. That is why she won't allow you to take another wife!"

"You are my wife in spirit! What more can I do if Sena doesn't ask the Brehons for a formal divorce or allow for another wife?" Father sounded exasperated.

"What more can you do? *You* can initiate divorce."

He said nothing.

Mother took a deep breath and continued. "You can tell me how you're going to explain this situation to Brigid. She already knows about Bacene. Sena told her, right there in front of the granary, in front of half the women in the tribe. Is that how you want your daughter to be treated?"

He sighed. "We were never planning to keep this situation a secret from Brigid. We wanted to wait until she was old enough to understand."

I was confused, not sure what I had witnessed, but felt some measure of relief knowing their secrets were not intentional. Father was going to tell me about his other family, full of sons.

"My concern is how Brigid will be viewed by everyone. She should be raised as a daughter of a druid, with status."

"I will always protect her," said Father.

"Will she be a slave? Or will she be a druid's daughter?"

My parents moved away from the door and continued a conversation that I couldn't hear. I picked up the bucket and went to the pigsty.

Of course I wasn't a slave. I was a druid's daughter.

CHAPTER 4

Patrick

The journey on the raider's currach was the worst experience of Patrick's life. He touched his raw neck, reddened from the iron chains that linked him to the two slave boys. Only a thin layer of damp stretched animal hide protected him from the gray sea, and each wave curved beneath him. His stomach lurched from motion and from fear, and he vomited over the side of the flimsy boat.

His unknown future terrified him. And his parents! They would return from Bannaven Taberniae and find him missing and the villa demolished. His father was Calpornius, a decuriones for Rome! He, as a tax collector, had clout! Maybe he could bargain with the Irish raiders. And what had happened to Linus? Patrick assumed his friend had run to get help. But what if he just ran? Worst of all, images of Siculus's violent death continued to flash before his eyes. Siculus, his friend. The servant who helped raise him from childhood. He felt sick, thinking of the Siculus's last undeserved wretched moments.

The bleak, gray sea that stretched out before him. Seamus, he noted, gave brief, harsh orders over the waves in Irish—most definitely the captain. The crew followed him without question. A group of girls huddled in the neighboring currach, much to the delight of the seamen.

"Hands off," Seamus called to his men as they ogled the women. "We want to fetch a good price for the ladies. Pure ladies," he added with a pointed look to his crew. Patrick sorted through his peculiar comprehension of the odd Gaelic. At least his fellow companions wouldn't be violated. Here, anyway. He had a soldier's training. He'd heard the stories. The inevitable was bound to happen.

The young women clutched at each other in the next boat, yet seemed unharmed. Patrick knew them all. There was Brawen, his half-Silurian neighbor. Her parents had a pagan-Christian romance of which his father disapproved. His goal was to stamp out the local Silures, those native tribes who still clung to pagan ways. Next were Darceca and Lupida, daughters of Roman officials in his villa. They shied away from the morning light and the stares of the sailors.

"Let them be," Seamus ordered again with a stern eye on his men. The three girls grabbed onto the side of the swaying boat for balance.

"Patrick!" Brawen cried out as she spied him across the water. Darceca and Lupida stifled their cries, and the four Britons reached to each other with their eyes over the sea-washed edge of the currach.

The boats moored against land, grinding into the sandy shoreline where the strand gave way to jagged cliffs of limestone and shale. Befuddled and exhausted after nearly two days in the cramped, narrow boats, Patrick stood, chained to the others, his legs aching and weak. Darys couldn't reach the currach's rim and had vomited in the boat instead. Patrick would have given anything for a hot Roman bath at Aquae Sulis, where his father had taken him for their family holiday last year. Darceca and Lupida, seasick even onshore, retched into the rising tide. Brawen stroked their backs as best she could confined in irons.

Patrick developed a new respect for the young women, whom a week before he considered rather silly. Darceca flirted with the Roman soldiers in training, while Lupida capitalized on her father's status, bragging about his wealth. Both he had found annoying as midges in the summertime, as they distracted his fellow soldiers from their drills.

Brawen was different. They had grown up together and Patrick particularly remembered their childhood summers spent in the river. Tough as any boy, she had dunked him beneath the Sabrina's murky depths as often as he dunked her. Her parentage was of the local Silurian tribe, one that Patrick, with his mixed Roman blood, eyed with suspicion.

Patrick kept quiet about the fact that his mother was a quarter Silurian because his grandmother, a full Silurian, had fallen in love with a Roman soldier. Patrick's sharp features mirrored his father's Roman aristocracy, while only the blue of his eyes reflected his ancestry from local Celtic tribes through his mother. She never spoke of this lineage. Brawen reminded him when he teased her. It made him distinctly uncomfortable.

Patrick's toes dug into the cold, clammy sand as he viewed the busy harbor. The smith's hammer on iron rang in rhythmic beats and sparks flew from his stall. Chained collars bound prisoners together while around them people traded their foodstuff and woolens. Slavery. His family owned slaves, usually those of the Pictish tribes. They were not free, but not poorly treated, either. He knew that in the heart of Rome, Celts were kept in captivity.

The concept of slavery, a practice the sixteen year old never thought about much, suddenly hit him, and he gasped at the realization of his destiny. He looked at Darys chained alongside him in a new light. Patrick glanced over at the girls. Darceca tended to Lupida, whose seasickness wouldn't leave her. He wondered if they knew what awaited them. Brawen did. Her eyes showed fear and her hands trembled, but he saw her take a deep breath of courage, determined not to show her fear to the wild Irish raiders. He vowed to do the same and face his fate with the same resolve.

The sailors unloaded the cargo, waiting to bring in their captives last. Perhaps they would all be sold together to one family, Patrick thought, or on neighboring farms. Perhaps there would be some way for them all to keep in contact.

"Wait, Fergus." Seamus stopped the sailor that had lined up the Britons. "All but these two stay here at Lambay." He unlocked the chains and pulled Brawen and Patrick back on the boat. They rubbed their sore necks and wrists. "These two are coming to Rathlin with me."

Fergus didn't question his captain's choices and bound Lupida and Darceca, as they shook with fear, to the rest of the captives, chained at the neck. They looked back at Patrick; their tear-filled eyes begged him to help, to set them free.

He rushed forward, impulsively. "Ní! cheadaíonn tú! Let us all... "

He stopped as he realized he had spoken Irish, not Latin or Welsh. He suppressed a chill of fear. Now, his captors knew he understood everything they said. Patrick pressed forward and grasped the edge of Lupida's woolen cloak. Seamus's huge fist slammed into his jaw, his futile rescue effort cut short. He fell onto the shore, and frigid seawater seeped through his leather breeches.

"Get going," Seamus ordered Fergus, while Brawen knelt beside Patrick and touched his face to gently check for a broken jaw. Seamus shoved her aside and spoke into Patrick's ringing ear.

"Don't try to be a hero, laddie. It's the way of the world." He reached down. Patrick winced, expecting another shocking blow. Instead, Seamus pulled him up by his grimy nightshirt collar and smiled at him in an almost friendly way. "Soon, you will have to tell me how you learned the Irish."

CHAPTER 5

Brigid

My mother avoided meeting my father's eyes and she turned away when he tried to speak to her. Lengthy silences settled as routine in our house. I kept to myself, organizing my rock collection and studying the different patterns of crystals, gazing into the quartzite interior. Finally, Father approached me, and we went to the pasture to sit upon my favorite stone.

"I want to tell you about the woman, Sena, who spoke to you."

I nodded, eager to hear the whole truth.

"Sena was once my wife. She wasn't a kind woman. Unfortunately, I didn't recognize this until after we were married. Your mother came to live with us, to help with the household chores." He paused, waiting to see if I understood.

"Mother was your servant?"

"She was. Brought in from a raid. I didn't plan for - well. When I tried to tell Sena about Brocca's pregnancy, she lost all reason. She refused to accept Brocca as a second wife. She refused to acknowledge or discuss any kind of divorce, although she asked me to leave our home, understandably. In compliance with the Law, I provide for her. I'm sorry if this is complicated, Brigid."

"Does that mean that boy is my brother?" I asked. That concerned me more than figuring out Brehon divorce law or understanding that Mother had been a servant in the past.

"Yes."

"I don't like him, Father. Bacene is always mean and dirty."

"I'm sorry for that, too, Brigid. He stayed with their mother, and she refused to let me raise him. However, I do support him and care for him in any way I can."

He talked about his love for Mother and me, and I believed him. But the incident with Sena reopened many unhealed wounds between my parents.

Maithghean visited soon after Father explained the situation to me. Carefully, he stepped around the colorful dye pots and skeins of wool that decorated our earthen floor. The chief druid looked at the copper pots and drinking horns hung from our ceiling racks with disdain, corners of his mouth turned down. The trappings of home and family seemed to make him uneasy.

"What can I do for you, Maithghean?" asked my father.

"I came to discuss the incident between the women."

Father winced and looked around. Mother was in the stables milking the cows. He knew the topic was still raw for her.

They sat across from each other at the table. I was on my pallet by the far wall, studying an amethyst nodule. Piles of folded wool hid me from their direct view. I think Father forgot I was there, or maybe he assumed I'd gone with Mother to the stables.

Maithghean spoke first. "This situation with Sena must be resolved. We can't have this conflict continue. It affects your work and your standing."

Father looked down and stared at his hands. "I won't give up Brocca. I consider her my wife."

"Maybe of the seventh degree," said Maithghean. Marriages were ranked by contracts and degrees. Father had tried to explain this to me earlier. If a man chose more than one wife, the wife of first degree would have seniority over the others, according to Brehon law. Sena didn't accept my mother as a second wife, and my parents' arrangement fit none of the Brehon's criteria.

"You know that situation is impossible," Father said through gritted teeth.

Maithghean shrugged. "You have sons with Sena that you barely recognize. Sons that could use a little discipline," he added. "You gained no property from Brocca. She owns nothing. You never had the Beltane ceremony. Brocca can't ever be a contract wife for you," he reminded Father coldly.

"You wouldn't *allow* a marriage ceremony for Brocca and me, influencing Dunlang and the other druids to back your position. As for the behavior of my sons, Sena refuses to let me see the boys and insists on raising them herself. I can't change the patterns she has begun."

"Brocca is a slave. A Pict. You bought her as a slave, and she remains in your household as one."

"She is free, according to this house."

"But not according to Dunlang, and he's the chieftain. Not according to Brehon Law."

Father ignored his comment. "She chooses to work with the animals. You know of the training she had in Alba, before she was taken."

"Her training must not have been terribly significant or the Picts would have tried to bargain for her," Maithghean countered, leaning over the table toward Father. "Trade is common; they could have pleaded her case if they chose."

Suddenly, Maithghean saw me crouched against the wall. He focused on my pile of stones. "Brigid, tell me about your collection."

I looked to my father. He nodded.

"Flint, quartz. Shells from the beach." I was relieved he asked me about my collection rather than the nightmares I had of the old Tuatha dé Danann gods and goddess.

"And what do you do with all of those stones?" He stared at me with uncomfortable attentiveness.

"Study them," I said. "I look at the different kinds of crystals in each one."

"Tell me more about the crystals, Brigid. Come here and show me." I walked to the table and placed a handful of rocks in front of Maithghean. My father watched but didn't say a word. I explained to Maithghean how I organized the rocks into categories and how I grouped them by the simple designs I saw within the rocks.

"What do you do with these two?" Maithghean quizzed me, holding up a chunk of flint and quartzite. Immediately, I struck them together. A tiny spark flew and the stones smelled of smoke.

Mother entered the house in the middle of my explanations. "What do you want with my daughter?"

"Calm down, Brocca," Father said softly.

"She already spends enough time following Elían around." Mother hovered at my side.

"Elían?" Maithghean raised an eyebrow.

"She teaches me about plants and medicines," I offered hesitantly.

"I see Brigid has great talent," Maithghean began. "Possibly, she has more potential than we know." He knelt down beside me, whiskers from his wild beard brushing across my cheek. "Tell me, Brigid, what stories do you know about the old gods?"

"Only the stories told at Midwinter." On cold winter nights, our tuath gathered in Dunlang's hall. Our neighbors took turns telling stories, but the ones about the ancients were reserved for the druids. Tagdh , an apprentice bard, wove tales of how Nuada lost his hand in battle, how the god Lugh rose bright in the sky with the morning sun. The stories were as familiar to me as any, and I could recite along with him.

"Your father says you have nightmares." Maithghean knelt down beside me so that we were level. "Tell me about your dreams. What do you remember?"

I stared at the floor. Something inside warned me not to tell him, not Maithghean, about my nightmares of the old gods who begged to be restored to the land. *Brigid! Help us! They pulled me to them and I sank into the earth. I couldn't move. I couldn't run. Brigid! My mother, but not my mother. A man with amber eyes grasped my ankle, pulled me into a thick bog. Set us free!* My own scream awoke me.

"Your father says that you call out for Macha," he prompted. I shot a look at my father, angry at his betrayal. "That you wake up screaming."

"Brigid, answer the chief druid," Father reprimanded.

I lied intentionally for the first time in my short life. "Sometimes I see fairies in my dreams. The Danann fairies are hiding under rocks."

"And this causes you to have nightmares?" Maithghean questioned.

"They pop out from under the stones and frighten me."

His eyes narrowed. He didn't believe me.

"What do you know about Macha or Dagda?" He put his hand on my forehead. I wanted to run away, but Father held me still. Maithghean reached for something, as if his hand reached inside of me, searching for my secrets.

"The bard's stories. I already told you that."

Maithghean touched the spot between my eyebrows, then placed his entire hand across my forehead. I felt the probing, the questions. I didn't know what he was trying to discover. Then I felt the pull of dreams returning to me, not of fairies, but the Old Ones trapped underground. He pulled the truth from me. I wouldn't tell Maithghean of my knowledge that the stories were more than stories. It was as if I knew the Old Ones as family, as friends.

"She is certainly more apt to follow in your footsteps, Dubhtach, than her foolish brothers." His yellow eyes peered into mine. He dropped his hand and kept his gaze on mine for a few seconds longer.

Maithghean left and a silence settled over us. Father looked at me, his brow creased. He ran his hand over my head, smoothing away the disgust that lingered from Maithghean's touch. "Brigid, what are you not telling me?"

CHAPTER 6

Patrick

Patrick watched helplessly as his fellow Britons, all except for Brawen, were marched away by force to the harbor square. Their hands were momentarily freed from the chains as Darceca, Lupida, and the rest were unshackled from them, bound again in a new line, and sent into the market. He lost sight of the people he had known his entire life. He reached for Brawen's hands.

The sailors looked toward Seamus to see if they should break up the reunion. Seamus shrugged and motioned for his men to chain the prisoners once again. Patrick flinched as the heavy irons pulled his arms slack in front of his body. A swift movement from a burly sailor shoved Patrick and Brawen, and they fell awkwardly, chained together, back into the boat.

The currachs retreated from the shoreline, and the sailors rowed at full strength. They traveled north, keeping the mainland in view.

Brawen stared at the thin oatmeal gruel the captain handed to them in rough, rotted wooden bowls.

"You must eat," Patrick encouraged Brawen. "Keep your strength."

"Why?" She flared up at him. "So I can be sold? Bear the children of some strange man?" Patrick knew that seeing her friends sold off the boats deflated her earlier resolution of courage. He hated to see his sprightly friend defeated.

"Perhaps..." Misty light shone through the clouds. That light gave him hope. And an idea.

"What is it?" Brawen urged him.

"Maybe we can escape, somehow."

"How?" Brawen's eyes gleamed, but then she held up her chained hands. Patrick didn't answer immediately. The hope in her eyes made his heart soar.

"Our next port is Antrim—Seamus has mentioned that it is his home—we can stowaway on a ship returning to Britannia."

"How will we know which ships are returning home?" Brawen lifted the bowl of oatmeal to her mouth.

Good, she's eating, Patrick thought.

"Romans trade all the time," he replied. "Surely, there will be a ship to return us to Britannia. We'll need to figure out how to slip past Seamus. You saw how chaotic it was when they unloaded cargo. It shouldn't be too difficult to slip onto another boat." He spoke quietly. While he didn't think these sailors knew Welsh, they were traders. They'd have to know a few words.

Brawen nodded in agreement.

"We'll need to save some food, if there is any bread to be had. Or, be prepared to go hungry." He gave her a pointed look. In his soldiers' training, he had gone without food for days. Womenfolk didn't.

"You'll need to learn a few words of Irish to help us escape." When Brawen's brows furrowed, he explained. "If other sailors catch you, it may be best if you can pretend to be Irish. There is a chance they would let you go."

"Patrick, how are we going to learn Irish?" She paused as if remembering the events of the morning. "You do speak Irish! How did you learn it?"

Patrick's face burned. He didn't know how he spoke it when he tried to save Lupida and Darceca. It came out of him, unbidden. Patrick knew the language. A cold shiver snaked down his spine.

Brawen waited for his answer. He resolved to put the thoughts out of his mind, at least until they were home. In safety, he could ponder this bewildering happenstance.

"Lessons. You remember my tutor, Dyfed? He taught me all sorts of languages."

She seemed to accept this explanation.

"Now, let's make our plan.

The currachs docked far to the north, at Rathlin Island.

"I'm always grateful, coming home, you know," Seamus remarked to Fergus. "The green hills, the cold air, never fail to invigorate me. Aye. I'd like to see my home, my flock of sheep, and my clansmen." They lifted sacks of grain out of the currach. Fergus replied in a low voice, something Patrick couldn't hear. His comment made Seamus shake with laughter.

"Oh yes, my wives as well! Two are all I can handle!" Seamus roared. He chuckled again and his eyes settled on Brawen. "Perhaps three wives would be bearable, aye Fergus?" Seamus leaned over the side of the currach and stroked a finger along the length of her braid. "She has lovely brown hair."

Brawen jerked away and Patrick tried to stand, but the chains pulled him down. Seamus grinned again and smacked his hands together as if in anticipation.

The crew dragged the currachs onto smooth shores outlined by ribbons of green. Seamus inspected his vessels for damage while the crew unloaded the final stacks of booty: redware plates, gold pieces, jewels, coins, and yards of silken goods.

Patrick and Brawen stayed in the boat at the far end, water lapping against the sides, watching the crew prepare for business. With nagging annoyance, Patrick listened as conversations swirled around him. The oat crops were bad this year and the wheat worse. From their gloomy talk, Seamus's people were close to starving during the cold, damp winter.

The sailors unloaded the grains, stolen from the storage bins of Bannaven Taberniae. Shouts greeted them when the crowd of local villagers spotted the barrels of food.

Seamus shouted above the din. "This here will be sold for a price."

"A fair price?" a man called, as Seamus hefted a sack of oats over his shoulder. "We had just as rough a winter as you."

Seamus glared at the man, who, in Patrick's opinion, looked fit and hale for all his complaints. Seamus ignored him and stacked the grain. The rest of the crew followed Seamus's lead and hauled and divided the wares among the carts that waited on shore. Seamus pulled a blade from his pocket to cut the ropes. With an unabashed gasp, Patrick saw that he held Sicilus's small copper knife.

Seamus glanced at him and shrugged. "No need to waste a good weapon."

Patrick looked to Brawen, whose wrists were raw from the chains. She was dressed in a rough spun wool shift and light slippers. He noticed that his leather breeches refused to dry. They were both filthy, covered in smoke and soot from their burning homes.

A sailor returned to the boat for more booty and noticed Brawen's bleeding wrists. He reached toward her, and she flinched, terrified.

"You aren't going anywhere." The sailor unlocked their chains and allowed them to stand. He led them to a pile of goods stacked on the sandy beach.

"Here," he said as he undid the heavy iron lock.

Patrick heard the sailor's words and understood them. He gritted his teeth against the unease that gnawed at the back of his mind. The sailor unsnapped the metal and wrapped a dirty rag around Brawen's forearm, then caught Seamus's glare. Hastily, he tied the two prisoners with thin rope, uncomfortable, but much more tolerable than the irons.

Brawen struggled against the ropes, but only succeeded in making her wrists more raw and painful. She cried out in frustration.

"Patrick," she whispered to him. "These ropes are bound too tight. We'll never escape!"

"Shh!" The last thing they needed was a sailor to walk by and hear her, even if she spoke in Welsh. "Remember, we must look defeated. Resigned. Stop struggling and the plan will work. Wait for my word."

They leaned against a barrel stacked alongside the currach.

"Soon, they will come for us. Study the port, the ships, the trade boats; let's see what may be to our advantage." He considered their meager belongings. He had managed to slip one hardened clay flask of fresh water, stolen from the sailor's rations, into his leather trousers, and Brawen had another tucked into a pocket in her shift. Still, two small canteens were not enough.

"Patrick, look!" Brawen nodded to the boat next to theirs. Patrick followed her gaze to the oak-hewn vessel and its crew, a sturdier-looking craft than the skin-covered currach. They were common folk, Silures from the west of his home. He had visited them once, with his father two summers ago on a trading mission. He recognized their strong Welsh, without a hint of Latin to taint the accent. Brawen smiled, indicating she had also heard the Welsh.

"It's a possibility, although I don't know if those men can be trusted any more than these Erin-men." All men, from whatever land they came, were dangerous to a lone woman on a boat.

He didn't want her to get her hopes up, yet even so, he started to contrive a more concrete plan. He considered the sailors at their chores. They could conceivably slip away onto the neighboring vessel. Could they throw themselves on the mercy of the Silures, Roman born and bred as they were?

Brawen interrupted his thoughts. "I don't care if they're not to be trusted. I want to go home," she said boldly. "I can wield a sword as well as you."

Patrick frowned and tried to discern her meaning.

"Brawen, those men—any men on these boats—could be unsafe for you."

She gave him a withering look that made him blink in surprise.

"Oh, please, Patrick! I know what could happen. Do you think we women are so stupid? And besides, I've been to the Beltane fires, if that's what your thinking." Her gaze turned to the Silures.

Patrick stared at her, speechless. Brought up in a Christian Roman household, he believed women were safe and sheltered. Women waited until marriage to be with a man. He heard the rumors about rampant sex at pagan festivals. Even he, at sixteen and with soldier's experience, hadn't yet...

"You went to the Beltane fires?" he asked, incredulous.

Brawen's impatient sigh made him feel very naive. "My mother is Silure, remember? We celebrate both the native and Roman festivals in my home." She seemed so matter of fact about the heathen traditions, the ones his father and his Christian colleagues worked hard to stamp out in their part of the island. He vaguely remembered Brawen's family traveling in the spring. He had always believed her father, a smith, went for the copper trade. To go to...? They let their daughter...?

"Brawen, how could you? How could your family let you? You'll be disgraced for your future husband!"

She glared at him. "I'm tired of your Roman propriety! Your beliefs are not the only ones in Britannia. Remember, the Silures, and our traditions, were here first!"

He saw that she considered herself full Silure, rather than the one-half she normally hid around her friends.

"Besides, you are not as Christian as you would like to seem, now are you?" Brawen continued her rant in a low, angry, whisper. "And it's not disgraceful! It's an honor. My future husband, a true British man—not Roman—will be proud!"

There had been more going on in Bannaven Taberniae than he knew. His father, a Christian deacon, told him that the heathens were nearly gone from the land, and Rome had accomplished its goal of Christianizing the local pagans.

Brawen tried to pull away but the ropes bound them. "Damn it!" she cursed.

Patrick was ashamed of his unintended insults, although shocked by what she told him. He knew their quarrel wouldn't help them escape. If they didn't find a way out soon, he would be a slave and Brawen would be servant and wife to Seamus. Honor would be meaningless.

His eye caught an edge of a copper metal band that protruded from the edge of a barrel. He touched the triangular point. Blood trickled in a thin line down his fingertip.

"Brawen, look."

Brawen followed his gaze and slowly, so as not to attract attention, they moved their bound hands to the barrel and then placed the rope that tied them together over the pointed metal.

"So, you want to get away from me this badly?" Brawen asked with a sardonic smile.

"We can discuss it on the way home, in that Silure boat. We'll be so busy talking that you won't have time to sell yourself to the sailors." Wrong thing to say. Patrick winced at the look on her face. His attempt at sarcasm failed.

Brawen's anger flared. "Patrick! I didn't say anything about selling myself! Just because I celebrated Beltane doesn't mean... " She seemed to recognize that such arguments were useless and took a deep breath. "All I mean is that I know what to expect. I know what could happen. I'm not an ignorant girl anymore. The chance of them hurting a fellow Silure is low. They may even know my father."

She had a point. Patrick decided to remain silent. He continued to saw the rope back and forth on the metal.

"Keep an eye on the Silure boat," he reminded her. Boats full of trade goods, the Silurian sailors untied ropes from posts that held their crafts to the shoreline and called orders to each other. Patrick wondered if there would be room enough for two stowaways.

A few tendons of the rope started to fray then, finally, break. The rope snapped.

"Here, Brawen, hold my hands. We have to make it seem our hands are still bound together. On my signal, we will run to the Silures. They're our only hope of getting home." Patrick caught her shudder as Seamus's huge bulk approached.

"Remember," Patrick steadied the anxious quiver in his voice. "Run quickly along the shoreline to the Silures, no matter what."

Seamus called orders. "Bring the gold to the chieftain. Take it now. You can't keep it, Fergus. The oats, the silks, the wool all go to the market."

Patrick and Brawen were the last of the cargo. He took a deep breath, said a silent prayer, then pushed Brawen in front of him.

"Go!" he hissed. She stumbled then ran, too sudden for the Irish sailors, burdened with their last load of grain. Patrick began his sprint and found his legs weak and cramped. A heavy hand on his collar yanked him back.

"Take me home!" Brawen cried in a perfect Silurian dialect as she ran up to the neighboring vessel. The Welshmen pulled her aboard.

Patrick struggled under Seamus's furious grip until a solid blow threw him dizzily into darkness.

CHAPTER 7

Brigid

One of my chores was to herd sheep from the fields, while my mother herded in the cows. I ran with springing steps over the moist turf. Our lambs had wandered farther than usual, edging along the rock-lined border between the grazing land and oak forest. I hopped on and off the rock border that separated the two. I balanced on a pointed stone and watched the sky soften into pink hues. I continued short, balancing steps along the stone fence, awed by the thick trees that blocked the light. I saw a flash of white robe and brush of movement. I was near the oak grove where the druids met to practice their secret rituals.

I glanced back at the sheep and lambs that cropped green grass in short, sharp bites. Curious, I looked again toward the forest interior. It wouldn't hurt if I went near...only to see the ritual. I promised myself that I wouldn't interrupt. After all, I was to be a druid one day. I should be able to watch their meeting.

My father rattled the throwing sticks within the circle of white-robed druids and read the portends. The circle listened, intent on his prophecy. I crouched behind a thick bush of hazel as a faint wave of guilt passed over me. I shouldn't be spying. The prophecies are for the entire village, I rationalized, not just the druids.

"Our people are hungry and the grain has rotted..." Father's voice retained a distant quality, as if he spoke from another place. "There will be a fierce battle, far to the south."

Maithghean questioned him. "Who is fighting in the battle? Is it the tribe of Fotharit?"

Silence. Father must have nodded his reply because I heard Elían's sharp intake of breath.

"We can't lose any more warriors," she said. "We have lost too many over the past raids."

"Warriors will be lost," Father intoned. "They're always lost in blood."

"Do we win?" Maithghean asked eagerly. "How many cows do we gain? How many prisoners?"

Elían interrupted. "We don't know when this will be. Our land is not yet bare. Listen to what the future holds before you begin gathering our spoils."

I had never heard anyone gainsay Maithghean.

Father, still in his seer's trance, predicted the warriors who would fall in battle.

"What battle is this?" Maithghean argued. "These are not men of our tribe!"

Still crouching, I stole toward the meadow where the sheep waited to be led home. A twig snapped under my knee as I moved to leave.

"What was that?" Maithghean asked.

Father halted his monotonous list of names. I froze. The hazel branches hid me. On my hands and knees, I curled to the ground and leaned my forehead on the leaf-matted soil.

"Who's here?" Maithghean called. It was a precarious point in the prophecy. The druids couldn't leave Father in his trance state, but I knew, if caught, my punishment would be severe.

"It's nothing, only an animal in the trees," Elían soothed.

"Let's continue," Tagdh added. "Or we'll lose Dubhtach in his trance."

Carefully, I crept out of the forest.

Each winter, we celebrated the ceremonies for Imbolc in the center of our village. The season had been long and damp. We were glad for a break in the monotony of gray. Imbolc celebrated the start of the lambing season, and it was one of my favorite festivals. It was a day dedicated to the Goddess Brigid, for whom my father named me. I imagined myself in swirling colors, able to blend in with the earth whenever I wanted, and I danced around with joy.

"This is my favorite day!" I declared happily to Mother as we walked from the farm. Father had left early for the oak grove to prepare.

"It's the day of your namesake," she said. "You stay close beside me, Brigid. Don't talk to Sena. Ignore her if she tries to talk to you." I hadn't forgotten the rude woman, who was still my father's wife, and her sons, who were my brothers.

The whole village was alive with activity. Brightly colored flags lined the booths in the marketplace. I wore the skirt of a druid's daughter, woven with bright colors, and a matching blue cloak lined with yellow and red. Mother tied my hair in elaborate braids for the occasion, fastening tiny gold balls to the end of each braid. I skipped through the túath, listening to the tinkle of my ornaments.

Mother helped other women cook for the feast, and a makeshift kitchen was organized in the center of the village. Wild game and mutton roasted in earthen pits. Vegetables and stews cooked in large cauldrons. I watched my mother as she set to her task. Her skirt was a rough weave. No colorful plaid. Only a dull bronze brooch clasped her cloak. Once again, her status was recognizable.

I turned away, ashamed. She wasn't any degree of wife to my father. Just his servant. A slave gotten from an overseas raid. I wouldn't let it ruin my day. I looked eagerly for Moina, my friend whom I met with at each festival. We played with her spotted clay marbles while our mothers prepared the feast.

"Brigid!" Moina called. She waved from her house. She lived within the ring fort. She didn't live on a farm as we did because her mother, Elían, was the healer. Her father had died, and her two older brothers were training to be warriors.

"Please, may I go?" Mother saw that my brothers were not nearby and allowed me to go. I ran ahead, blue cloak flying behind me, not caring about the mud on my calfskin boots. Moina and I joined hands. We believed we were soul friends, *anam cara*, souls bound to lifetimes together.

"Moina, aren't you excited about Imbolc? It's my favorite day!"

"Yes, I know you have the same name as the goddess Brigid," she said impatiently. "Everyone knows your father named you after her. Look, I have the marbles." We sat in the doorway to play and to still see the excitement of the festival.

"One day, I will be a healer," I stated as she knocked another one of my pieces out of place.

"Not me," she said. "I don't want to be around sick people all the time. I want to live on a farm. We should change places."

"I like our farm, but I want to be a druid, too, just like my father." We continued our game, and Moina told me stories of helping her mother stitch sword wounds on the bleeding stomach of a dying warrior.

"So far, Elían has only shown me plants and herbs. I don't know how to stitch _"

A dirty foot kicked our marbles through the doorway, leaving a brown smudge on the white lime. It was Bacene. My brother.

"Go away," I told him. Moina scowled and collected her scattered toys.

"I don't need to do anything you say, little Brigid. Who cares that you have a festival with your name on it!" He stuck out his tongue.

"It's my festival and it's my day, so leave us alone!"

"It's not your day. You're not the Goddess!" Bacene sneered.

Moina ran across the marketplace to get our mothers. I stood to follow her, but Bacene blocked my way. "Move!" He refused, stepping left then right. Bacene reached for my braid and pulled it, snapping off one of the golden ornaments.

"Stupid red—fire hair!" He yelled, making fun of my copper curls.

Tears brimmed in my eyes, and anger welled with red heat to the top of my skull. I hated this boy. I didn't care if he was my brother or not.

I reached out and poked him in the eye. Bacene cried in pain.

"Brigid scratched my eye!" he yelled. The women cooking around the cauldron heard our cries. Sena and Mother ran to separate us and then glared at each other.

"What did your filthy son do to my daughter?" Mother hissed at Sena.

"Your daughter has blinded my son!" she yelled in return.

Onlookers must have sensed a brawl and sent for our father while our mothers hurled obscenities at each other. Father came running and Maithghean followed close behind him.

Father was at a loss, poised between both Bacene and myself. He didn't know which child to comfort first. Bacene yelled louder.

"She said she was a goddess! She punched me in the eye!"

"He pulled my hair!" I fired back, annoyed that Father stood by his worthless son instead of me. "And give me back my jewelry!" I yelled as he pocketed the tiny gold ball.

Maithghean, with his penetrating yellow eyes, knelt down next to me. "Did you say you were a goddess, Brigid?"

I refused to answer and stared at the mud-soaked ground.

"Remembering a past life could lead to very special powers," he pressed, whispering into my ear. "Don't you want to show that brat Bacene what gifts you possess?"

His hand grasped my arm and I felt that pull that left me short of breath. It was as if the chief druid tried to pull my soul from me. I looked up and met his eyes that seemed to glow from within. I imagined what it would be like to unleash goddess powers on Bacene. He wouldn't bother me ever again. I giggled at the thought of his dirty, scowling face running away in fear. Maithghean's long beard lifted at the corner in a hint of a smile.

"Leave the child alone." Mother yanked my arm from the chief druid's grasp. "Brigid only meant she shares the same name as the goddess."

"Is that so?" Maithghean's eyes followed as Mother pushed me toward the cooking pots and Father returned Bacene to Sena.

The druids began the solemn Imbolc ritual. They wore ceremonial cloaks and formed a semi-circle at the clearing in the village center.

"We grow in light because of Brigid, the *breo-saigit*, who brings the light, the fiery arrow," Maithghean called to the assembled tribe. He lit the kindling as it grew into a bonfire in the interior of the circle.

I stood with my hand in my mother's, watching the druids invoke the Goddess Brigid on Her day. We celebrated the new light as winter loosened its grasp on our land.

I had spied on the druid's rehearsal the day before in the oak grove. Hiding behind the hazel brush became a regular activity for me. Despite Mother's admonitions, I couldn't stop myself. Fascinated by druid work, I studied every ritual they rehearsed and memorized each chant. This is what I will do, I thought. The ceremony flowed with grace and beauty before our tuath. I will become a druid.

Father continued. "It's the time when the ground is furrowed for seeds. The land will be ready to sow, and we will plant. Brigid awakens new life in the cold earth, as shown by the new life in your flocks." He held up a newborn lamb. There would be no sacrifice at this ceremony; it was one to celebrate life. I found myself murmuring the sacred words along with the druids. A surge of energy raced from my feet through the crown of my head; energy from the earth. Wooden cups of ewe's milk passed hand to hand so that each member of the tuath received a communal sip, uniting the people of Fotharit as one tribe.

"May the Goddess Brigid bless the fertility of our land and of our people. May she bless our bards with the gift of poetry and song. May they proudly speak the name of our chieftain to all corners of Éire!"

Mother's hand gripped mine. The crowd followed Dunlang out of the ring fort and into the fields, where he dropped the first seeds into the freshly plowed earth. The people cheered. Shivers ran through my spine, as I had a glimmer of memory, as if I had watched this ritual many times before.

CHAPTER 8

Patrick

Patrick awoke, packed in between barrels and bags of grain. His head pounded. He was chilled and achy, dampened by a soft sheen of rain that misted over him.

What happened? Patrick last remembered Brawen climbing aboard the Silure boat. She had made it. From the bow she had called to him, but Seamus had him firmly in his grasp.

"You're not going anywhere," Seamus had growled. Patrick twisted so he could see Brawen and reassure himself that she was safe. She waved frantically; the Silure sailors must have cut the ropes from her hands immediately. They were busy pushing off from the harbor, at risk of an unpleasant incident. A few of the Irish raiders had seen her escape and looked toward Seamus for direction.

Patrick didn't know if Seamus's clenched jaw meant anger or embarrassment, but he had watched with relief as Brawen headed toward home. Then, Seamus struck him on the back of the head, knocking him unconscious.

That explains the headache, he thought as the wagon continued its bumpy ride. He tried to sit up and get his bearings, but the wagon was too wet. His bare feet slipped over the wooden planks, adding splinters to his collection of wounds. He cried out, knocking his head back onto a sack of flour.

"You're awake then, lad, are you?" A strange voice rang out from the front of the wagon. Patrick didn't answer. It wasn't Seamus. He had been sold to someone else.

"Well," the man continued talking cheerily, "Welcome to Connacht. The greenest hills of   Éire are here. You will be enjoying yourself. It won't be too bad, I promise you that." The man whistled while Patrick jounced back and forth. He raised his head once more and was able to see a snatch of green before he was jolted again, head rocking side to side in throbbing pain.

Patrick lay back on the sack of grain, resolving to move as little as possible. He wondered what this man had in store for him. Servitude of some kind, he was certain, either physical labor in the fields or as a manservant. He wished he knew how long he had been unconscious. Then he could measure how far to the harbor. How could he escape from the middle of nowhere? The clouds obscured the sun, making it impossible to tell the time of day. He didn't know whether they traveled east or west.

Soon, the cart stopped its tormenting journey. He heard voices, a woman's, and small children. They were speaking in Irish, yet Patrick understood their entire conversation. This unsettled him, but now wasn't the time to ponder.

"Maura, I've come with supplies and some extra help."

The man began unloading the cargo. "This is for me to take to the village tomorrow."

A barrel moved and Patrick's wedged position shifted.

"And this," he continued, "is for you to keep." The grain sack beneath Patrick's feet slid out from under him, and his bare foot thumped the planks of the cart. A bolt of Roman silk was removed, and Patrick was exposed and alone in the wagon. A small hand tugged at his toes.

"What's this, Milliuc?" A boy asked.

Milliuc hopped in the wagon and pulled Patrick up by the collar of his tunic. Patrick stood and saw a small thatched hut, round and whitewashed, and a larger, round house nearby. A woman, Maura, he guessed, was dressed in a plain wool cloak and skirt. The two boys watched him intently.

"He's our new shepherd." Milliuc spoke to the youngest child, a boy of about five.

"What's your name? Where are you from?" The young boy pulled at Patrick's tunic. Patrick was about to answer when Milliuc spoke first.

"Ah, wait, Nial. He doesn't know Irish yet, do you? What's your name?" Milliuc poked him in the chest. "Your name?" he repeated in Irish, jabbing him again with a pointed finger.

"Patrick," he croaked, his throat dry with nervousness. Milliuc glanced sideways at him. Patrick wondered if Seamus had told him about the incident on the ship.

"What kind of name is that?" the boy questioned. "I can't say it."

"Some Roman name, Nial. We'll find a decent Irish name for him soon enough."

Milliuc pushed Patrick toward the edge of the wagon and motioned for him to follow Maura.

Maura entered a hut opposite a large circular house. Patrick supposed the house was Milliuc's. Woven together with twigs and mud and thatch, it was three times the size of the hut. Surrounding it were storage sheds, stables, and pens for the animals. Waterproofing reeds roofed all of the buildings, which sloped to allow the constant drizzle to drain. Sharpened posts enclosed the farm, and Patrick guessed it was both fencing and defense for the small landholder and his slaves.

Patrick found the interior of the slave's hut to be similar to those of the peasant farmers who lived on the outskirts of Bannaven Taberniae. It was simple but clean. A rough wooden bench served as the only seating, and in the corner was a woman's loom for weaving. He noticed a tiny female figurine in a niche above the loom; he had heard how primitive the Irish were. A copper pot of boiling stew on the hearth reminded him that he was hungry.

"Liam, run and fill this with water." Maura handed a wooden bucket to a sullen-looking boy of about eight or ten. He dragged his feet until Milliuc gave him a swift whack on the back of the head, and Liam scuffled out the door. Patrick sat with exhaustion on the wooden bench and waited for his headache to subside.

"I'm going to get old Dathi. The new slave is in your hands." Milliuc left. Maura watched him leave.

Patrick wondered who Dathi was, but busied himself eating the mutton stew Maura set before him. It was delicious. Young Liam had brought back the water, and Patrick drank mouthfuls from the dipper.

He took another gulp of stew, appreciating the onions and meat, when he realized he could escape. Milliuc was gone. Maura had turned her back and was showing the youngest boy how to skin a slaughtered sheep properly.

Patrick looked around and nervously wiped his sweaty palms on his tunic. He hooked the water bucket over his elbow and stuffed a couple of onions from the tabletop into his tunic pocket. Unconscious during the journey from the harbor, he didn't know which direction to go or how long it would take. He was thankful to his Roman legionnaire who taught the young boys of Bannaven Taberniae how to run for miles, build a campfire, and hunt wild game. Standing, he winced from the pain of splinters in his heels. His sandals had disappeared after leaving the raiders' boat.

He crept to the door, easing open the oak on silent leather hinges. Outside, he stared at the mist rolling in and he paused, uncertain. The thick low cloud could help conceal him for an escape—or he could become hopelessly lost.

Patrick knew the fog most likely came from the sea, so he would head straight into the mist. He ran on the dirt path that took him here, wherever "here" was.

Running blindly, he ignored the stones that demolished his feet. The bucket sloshed and Patrick hoped enough water remained to quench his thirst. The vegetables in his pocket banged against his hip. He ran toward freedom.

Voices. Over the sound of his panting breath, Patrick heard voices. The mists made it impossible to tell if they were nearby or far away. He slowed in the whiteness and edged off the side of the road, listening for more clues.

It was Milliuc's voice, he could tell. Damnation! His heart pounded. Another voice, quieter and soft-spoken. It must be Dathi, who Milliuc went to retrieve.

Patrick backed off the path even farther until he felt a boulder behind him. The water bucket knocked against it, and he set the bucket down. Pressed up against the rock, he prayed to God that the farmer would pass by and not see him.

"I returned from this trip a rich man, Dathi," Milliuc said. "I hope that you will bless the merchandise for a good sale and prosperous crops for the farmers. We have more than enough grain to stave off any famine."

Patrick strained to see through the cloud but couldn't.

"It's up to the gods," said Dathi. "I'll check your grain, but we don't know if the seed is spoiled. Then, I'll talk to all the druids tomorrow in the oak grove."

They *are* pagan barbarians here, Patrick thought. They still have the old druid order. He believed the druids erased in most of Britannia, Brawen's family notwithstanding. Patrick lay low behind the rock. Having Milliuc find him and probably beat him would be bad enough; to have some spell cast on him by this foreign druid petrified him.

The sound of stumbling and a crash interrupted their casual talk.

"What in the name of Éire!" Milliuc yelled. "I fell atop this." He picked up the object that made him lurch, and Patrick heard the sloshing sounds of water. Oh, no. He had set the bucket on the ground.

"I made this jug! How did it get here?" Milliuc held it in front of Dathi.

"A mysterious omen," Dathi replied. Patrick held his breath, sure that the druid knew exactly where he was.

Milliuc thrashed along the path, kicking rocks in anger, frustrated with the dimness of light. "No, this is no omen, druid. This is my water pitcher, which was in my servant's house a short time ago." Pebbles sprayed Patrick's side.

"That boy!" Milliuc exclaimed. "That boy escaped!"

"What boy?" Dathi asked. "You failed to mention you brought back slaves."

"Only one," he grumbled. "Maura's children are old enough to work now, but I need to send someone out to the pastures. They'll all pitch in for the sheep shearing. Damn that woman. I'll beat her for her carelessness. I need this boy as a shepherd."

The silence deepened. Patrick began to wonder if they had left, but no, they were waiting for him to make a sound. The next thing he knew, Patrick was staring into unfathomable eyes surrounded by a white hood.

"We've been looking for you, dear boy," the druid said in Irish and then switched to Latin. Patrick bit his tongue to keep from replying, shocked that this man knew his language. The druid's hand encircled his wrist. He knew there would be no escape. "Milliuc, I believe I have found your slave boy."

Milliuc growled—a sound to which Patrick had grown accustomed—and grabbed his other arm.

"He's mine, Dathi!" Patrick was pulled between the trader and the druid. The druid won.

"I'll hold onto him," Dathi said. "What is his name?"

"Some kind of Roman rubbish," Milliuc sneered. "Patricius. Patrick. Padraic, in proper Irish."

Dathi smiled. "I'll consult with the druids."

Fear rose in Patrick's belly again. He had heard stories about human sacrifice among the barbarians. Even those in Britannia, like some of Brawen's ancestors, had practiced such rituals of death. *Even some of your own ancestors*, a quiet voice whispered in his mind.

It was as if Dathi had read his thoughts. "Don't worry, young one. We do no such things in Éire. You will be returned to Milliuc soon enough." His clairvoyance shook Patrick to the core.

CHAPTER 9

Brigid

As Father had predicted, our warriors were victorious when they stole cows from across our borders. We ended the next several summers by incorporating the prisoners of war into our tuath.

Mother and I walked to the ring fort with our heavy baskets full of eggs. We would trade our eggs for grains and other goods. I looked forward to purchasing herbs for new dyes, like indigo. I loved exploring the new colors to dye our wool with and admired my own skirt, brilliant with the seven colors of a druid's daughter.

While in the market, I recognized Lomman, whose family was among the prisoners from this summer's cattle raids, now servants to Dunlang, the chieftain.

"Hello, Lomman," I said while our mothers went about their business. I ventured a smile at the thin boy, all bones sticking out from a pale mop of hair and even paler eyes. He nodded. Clinging to his hands were his younger sisters, two tiny girls weakened from malnutrition. The whole family was hungry.

Granted a small plot of land by Dunlang, they were officially his servants and had to give a portion of their harvest to him. They couldn't leave Fotharit without Dunlang's permission. Lomman's father died soon after that raid, the result of an unhealed sword cut to his leg. His mother, Una, was given only a few chickens and a pig. I thought of our shed full of food, wheels of cheese Mother and I had, extra grain stored as the druid's share.

Una showed Mother thin cords of flax, which she must have gotten from women at the granary. She tried to barter it for our eggs. Her skirt was plain gray plaid, like Mother's, like all the women servants.

"We need no flax," Mother said. "We have enough of our own." She may have been in the same rank, but she had the advantage of living with a druid.

"It's all I have," Una whispered. "Please, a few eggs for my children. Our hens are old. They haven't set in days."

I pulled a small loaf of bread from my pocket, my lunch for the walk home, and gave it to Lomman and his sisters. They each grabbed at it, so I added cheese to their fare as well.

Mother saw me. "Brigid! Come here immediately!" I was nearing womanhood by then and didn't appreciate being scolded like a child. "Don't speak with those children! They're beneath you." She pointed to the plaid of my skirt and the plainness of theirs. Lomman and his mother reddened in embarrassment. I couldn't believe my mother. She was no different than them, a slave herself.

Rebellious, I glared at Mother. I picked up a basket containing two-dozen eggs and shoved it at Una. "We have plenty more eggs to trade. Take these." Both women stared at me. I had never intentionally disobeyed my mother before, but I refused to let this family go hungry.

"Brigid," Mother's voice was tight. "Those are all the eggs we have for today. We haven't anything else to trade."

"We don't need anything. We have a pot of dye, which is enough for Father's new cloak. Our shed is stacked with cheese. They are hungry."

My mother wanted to salvage what was left of her pride, but I wouldn't give in. As we engaged in a battle of wills, with Una standing awkwardly in between, Bacene raced past.

"Ha-ha!" he called. "Look at my new cloak!" He did, indeed, have a splendid new cloak that matched the woven plaid of my skirt. We were both children of a druid. It gave me an idea, a way to end my present standoff.

I turned to my mother. "I'm of the druid class," I said with unbelievable audacity. "You are not. Give the eggs to this family."

She paled and her hands gripped the basket, knuckles white.

I hated to use this newfound power of rank over my own mother, but she was trying to use what little she had over those even more poor. It was a sickening display of hierarchy.

Mother released her hold on the basket.

"Thank you, Brigid," Una said. "My children won't forget your generosity." She hurried away, leaving me to face my mother's wrath.

She didn't chastise me as I thought she would—which I rightly deserved. Instead, my mother allowed me to wallow in my own guilt. I hated that I had used superiority over her, yet I wouldn't apologize. She had tried to use hers over Una.

"Mother?" I tried to get her to speak to me. We kneaded dough and our hands met accidently as we worked. She pulled away.

"I have work to do in the barn," she said, leaving me alone.

I asked my father about it that evening when we walked through the meadow toward the stones where we spent hours in meditation.

"I couldn't help it, Father. I couldn't let Lomman and his family starve, and Mother wouldn't trade with them!"

Father held my hand. "It was noble of you to help, Brigid, but you should not ever disobey your mother, especially in front of others."

"Una and Mother are both slaves—Mother should sympathize with her."

We climbed onto the granite boulders warmed by the sun.

"Brigid, in her own land, your mother enjoyed rank and privilege. By bad luck and misfortune, raiders abducted her. Perhaps she was even more unfortunate to meet me. I haven't made her life easy."

"Father! You love her. You gave up Sena for her."

"There are many other things your mother must endure. Understand it is difficult for her."

"What was her rank in her homeland?"

"I will leave that story to her to tell in her own time. Brigid." Father turned to me. "You do understand the Law, regarding your position, don't you?"

"Yes, of course." I listened to his intonations many times as he recited family histories. I knew that he was of druid rank, mother was a servant, and by Brehon Law, he was required to take care of me, as his child.

"The sun is bright today," Father hastily changed the subject and introduced his lesson. The bright light was rare. "We shall contemplate Lugh, the ancient sun god. Perhaps the sun's warmth will bring us a prosperous harvest."

We closed our eyes, summoning our energies from the earth.

The sharp autumn wind was nothing compared to the bitterness of my mother's silence. Weeks passed without speaking until one blustery day my mother and I tended to a sick ewe. She was speaking to me again, although in brief spurts of necessary conversation. Our hands met across the belly of the dying sheep.

"I was once training to be a healer in my own land, Alba, across the sea," she began. "A druid healer." She paused when she saw the look of surprise on my face. She will finally tell me, I thought. She will let me know about her past.

"My parents thought I had the makings of a healer because I had such a way with animals. I would bring home injured rabbits and the like." She had coaxed the ewe to drink a few laps of water, her hand resting on the animal's belly, bloated with illness. "For two years, I studied, just like your father did. We learned many of the same things. The Picts are not so different from the Irish. They look different, smaller, darker, but they also believe in the powers of nature."

"Why did you stop your training?" I asked, knowing that decision altered her life forever. Had she continued druid studies, she would have been too valuable to be kidnapped. Raids between the two lands happened often; however, those of a higher class were usually protected. Mother stroked the curly wool of the sheep.

"My love is for animals. I didn't want to be a human healer. All of the star patterns, herbal brews, healing techniques that I learned, I applied to animals. If I had finished my druidic training, I would have had to work with humans, and for that I had no desire."

She stood. "This ewe won't live through the morning. Whatever the illness in her gut will taint her meat as well. Watch the flock when you take them to pasture, Brigid. They may have found a patch of poisonous herbs. Look for the purple flowers and pull as many as you can."

I followed her through the barn, a million questions biting at my tongue.

"Would you change your decision if you could?" I couldn't imagine giving up the opportunity for learning. I had been meditating on the granite stones with

Father my entire life. I knew how to read the energy of the earth and how to pre-dict the weather. Best of all, I knew the properties of stone and had accumulated so many that a wall formed around my bed.

Mother didn't answer my question but continued her story. "It doesn't matter. Not too long after, I was kidnapped by raiders along the coast, a common practice. They sent me to your father's house as a slave. He saw my true gifts, and I was grateful he saw those talents. He saw what was beyond my life as a servant, which is why he gave me the animals and the land here."

She looked around the farm as if content with the knowledge that her life's work had been successful. Father had left his luxurious high-ranking druid's house with Sena to give my mother the entire farm of sheep, pigs, and cows to care for and tend to.

We left the ewe alone and went to do the milking. Mother leaned against the red-eared cow as she milked, and I contemplated what she would do when that animal went on to its next life.

"Do you ever wish you could go back to your people?" I asked. She smiled and then paused. Her silence went on too long for me to feel comfortable. "Did you know that your great—grandmother was a clan chieftain? She led numer-ous battles and was famous throughout Alba. We were a small but proud clan. My grandmother won us land, cows, and respect." Although women could be druids, I hadn't known any as warriors. I hadn't known my ancestors bore a clan chieftain.

Mother stroked the red ears of her white cow and thought better of it.

"Mother, why can't you regain your status? Why are you still seen as Father's servant?"

She continued to stoke the cow, lost in thought. "I wish it were simple, Brigid, but it is not. If I could marry your father as a first or second contract wife, then my status would be solidified. Sena fights that, even to her own embarrassment. If Maithghean didn't hate me, he could persuade the Brehons to allow our marriage and thus raise my rank. That won't happen."

"Why does Maithghean hate you? Why wouldn't he want to help Father?"

"I have known Maithghean for many years, since I was brought to this land. Now that you are almost a woman, I suppose I can tell you the entire story."

I sat on the milking stool to listen.

"My people, the Picts, are across the sea in Alba. You know this already. When I was brought here, people hated me because I was from another land."

"But they took you!" I objected.

"It doesn't make sense. Maithghean was one of those people who looked down upon me, because I'm a Pict—small, dark. Look at you, Brigid: you have inherited my stature, but have your father's copper hair and fair skin. No one would ever know." I looked at my arm, white and scattered with freckles.

"When I became pregnant with you, Dubhtach's marriage to Sena was already over. She had left the house to stay with her mother, only as a trial separation. After all, she wasn't going to give up the status of being a druid's wife so easily. And, now you know, she has not. Dubhtach, of course, told Maithghean about his predicament. At first, Maithghean was sympathetic, but when he discovered I was pregnant, he was furious with Dubhtach. Furious about how his actions would reflect upon the Order. So, he offered to take me. He offered to buy me from Dubhtach and raise you as his own."

Loathing welled in my chest, and a ring of angry energy circled my skull.

"Do you mean Maithghean could have been my foster father?" His eerie yellow eyes would follow me, watch me. I often turned around in time to see him walk another direction. Disgust burned within me.

"Brigid, are you feeling well? There seems to be…" Her voice trailed off and she reached toward my brow, which pulsated with heat.

I pulled my cloak over my head. "I'm cold, Mother. Just a bit of a chill is all. Please, tell me more about Maithghean."

She glanced at me oddly and then continued her story. "I knew this would disturb you. You care as little for Maithghean as I do and you are right not to trust him. He tried for several months to convince me to leave your father. He even offered me my freedom. I loved Dubhtach and distrusted Maithghean even more. I was willing to stay under whatever circumstances."

"Why do we not live in the druid's circle of houses now? Why is Sena in Father's druid house?" I asked. "Why are we outside the village on the farm?"

"You know the Law. She has a right to that house inside the fort. Neither of them has formalized a divorce, and Dubhtach has not asked her to leave it. He committed adultery with me. It doesn't matter how bad their marriage was, she has the right to keep the house to raise her sons. Dubhtach's sons." She was tired of the saga. "Like I said before, your father bartered for this farm so I could have some peace and take care of the animals." Mother leaned on the cow for comfort as she always did, her sad brown eyes webbed with lines. She lived for Father's love, and yet it wasn't enough.

CHAPTER 10

Patrick

Patrick sat on the hillside, cold and shivering. The dampness seeped into his bones and the chill was permanent. He glanced around for the sun, but was reminded that it didn't exist when the mists rolled in.

"Céad míle faílte," Milliuc had said after Patrick returned from his summons by the druids, an interrogation by Dathi and the rest he'd rather soon forget. A hundred thousand welcomes. "You're in charge of these animals," said Milliuc. He pointed to the sheep in the pen and showed him the tool shed for the shearing. Patrick was sick to his stomach. He had no idea how to shear a sheep or herd them from one place to the next. He had never been responsible for the animals in his father's villa. That was the servants' job.

Milliuc had opened the gate to the pen and allowed a few of the lambs to run outside. They scampered through the grass.

"Go fetch them," he ordered Patrick, who stared dumbly after them. "Go!" Milliuc pushed him forward, and he began to run after the lambs. Humiliated and red-faced, Patrick ran in circles after the small animals, who bleated and baa-ed whenever he came near. It was clear he would need help in returning the lambs to the pen.

Maura, Liam and the others had come outside to watch his humiliation.

Finally, Milliuc allowed Liam to step in. "Show Patrick how it works, boy!"

The ten-year-old deftly cornered the lambs, and, as a group, herded them back home. Patrick was exasperated. It wasn't his fault he never had to deal with sheep.

He was to be a Roman official. He spent his mornings learning history with Dyfed, his afternoons in practice drills with the soldiers.

"Get on in there." Milliuc shoved Patrick into the pen. "Time to water them." He gestured to the large water barrel and motioned to pour the contents into the watering trough. Patrick, fatigued from everything, could not lift the barrel. Liam ran to assist him, but his mother held him back.

"He's got to learn to do it on his own," whispered Maura to her son, her eye bruised from a recent blow. She'd learned not to let Patrick out of her sight.

Patrick struggled with the water while the men laughed. He knew they could tell from his clothing, filthy as it was, that he was a high-bred Roman. Serves him right to do a little hard work, he heard them say in Irish. The entire farm community, owner and slaves, watched and jeered.

Patrick managed to shove the barrel in the right direction and tried to ignore the splinters multiplying in his hands, rarely touched by hard labor. He was frustrated that he could not accomplish the task of children, and doing this task was to be his fate.

"Dear God," he whispered in prayer. Finally, he pushed the barrel and tipped it so that the water poured into the lambs' trough. The thirsty animals lapped greedily after their long wait.

Liam broke free from his mother's arms. He ran inside the shed and returned with a wooden pail.

"Let me show you," he said to Patrick, who was now mortified beyond words. The child dipped the pail into the barrel and poured the water into the trough. Patrick hadn't even considered looking for a way to scoop out the water. He leaned against the straw thatched wall, on the verge of fainting.

"Maura, take him in. Let him rest for the night. Tomorrow, Liam can show him where to take the sheep to pasture."

The furnishings inside the slave quarters were sparse and minimal. Behind the wooden table was the sleeping area, and Maura divided off areas for herself and her children with curtains, leaving the men far against the wall. Patrick looked around at his new home. He wondered if he would ever see the villa again with the room he had to himself, filled with silk cushions and piles of blankets. He lay down on the single rough wool blanket and straw Maura had given him, pushed in between the other men's bedding. He turned to his side and studied the thatched branches that made up a thin wall and the tiny spiders residing within.

Eamon and Conall worked with the cattle and the planting. Although they were servants themselves, they took pride in their jobs and laughed derisively at Patrick. Not only did they laugh at his ignorance, they knew caring for the sheep was a lowly job, often something reserved for children.

"Tell us, Roman, how did you manage to get kidnapped?" Eamon asked, nudging him with a dirty toe. Patrick pretended not to hear.

Conall took pity on him and pushed Eamon aside. "Ah, leave him be for now. The lad's had a rough couple of days."

Patrick discovered he would have significant amounts of time alone as a shepherd. He swallowed hard when Milliuc told him of his duties, curious as to why he would receive such a task when he obviously knew nothing about animals. Milliuc continued speaking in Irish, using hand gestures to make his instructions clear.

Patrick pretended slowness, irked that he knew every word this man was speaking. Once again, he pushed the mystery of language out of his mind.

Milliuc continued. "You'll spend the next several weeks in the hills, until the end of the summer months. Then you'll return here to help with harvesting the crops. You will watch over the births of the new lambs in the winter. Come spring, you do the shearing then bring them out to pasture when the weather warms." Milliuc owned a stretch of farmland between the forest and the western sea, most of it covered with sheep and cattle. And now Patrick was being cast out from the farm and sent to the pastures. He almost laughed. Surely he could escape easily, far away from the farm and the village.

Liam accompanied him and several dozen sheep up the hill, showing Patrick the hut that was to be his shelter for the summer. It was nothing more than a small thatched shed next to the animals' pen. The two structures looked remarkably similar, Patrick thought with disdain.

"Now, the sheep only stay in the pen if the weather is bad or you notice some scavengers roaming about," Liam explained, pointing to the stone enclosure around the structure.

"Scavengers?" Patrick repeated the unfamiliar term. He knew the word, but he wanted to know what to expect.

"Predators," Liam explained. "Usually foxes, which you should be able to scare off easily enough. Occasionally wolves. We don't see them often, but you never know." Wolves? Patrick shuddered. With bow and arrow, he had hunted deer and hares in Britannia, but rarely encountered a predator. The few he had seen were from a distance, requiring no weapons aimed. How was he supposed to protect himself, or the sheep? He had a walking stick and meager supplies.

"Over here." The boy bounded through the grass. "See this set of stones here?" He pointed to a line of rocks centered through the field. "Milliuc likes to keep the sheep in a paddock. So, this summer they'll stay on this side of the border. It's your job not to let them run loose."

Patrick nodded, pretending to understand the hand gestures. He had no idea how to prevent farm animals from stepping over those rocks.

"Next summer," Liam continued. "You'll move them over to the next paddock, and so on. Otherwise, they will eat all the grass in one summer's grazing. Keep an eye out for those that are sick. Milliuc culls them out of the flock."

Patrick wondered why he had this job and not Liam himself. He supposed he was too young to stay on his own.

The boy stayed with him for three days, until Patrick performed the job to his satisfaction, then left for the farm. "Good luck to you, Patrick. *Slán leat,*" Liam called as he departed. Patrick looked to see if warriors or guards were watching them. He saw none.

Patrick nodded, still unsure whether to speak Irish or not. He had only managed a few halting words in his days with Liam, pretending to learn the language slowly.

"Be careful," Liam called, as he headed down the hillside. "There are spirits, na daoine sí, in the hills. They'll play tricks on you."

Na daoine sí? Patrick recognized the word but had to think about the translation. Fairies. Sprites. Liam warned him about the mythical things. Patrick laughed to himself, breathing in the cool, damp air, and for the first time in his life, he was utterly alone. He sat for a few minutes, exploring the silence.

Milliuc had provided him with a grimy wool blanket, a sack of flour, a few clay pots, and an empty water bag. Stacked along the wall were logs for a fire. The hut was barely large enough for him to stand in. By stretching his arms, he touched the opposing walls, such as they were. He didn't press too hard, afraid the dilapidated structure would fall.

Patrick made a bread-like concoction with the flour and water and heated it over a small fire. It was the first time he cooked for himself, and the results were not pleasing.

No other humans were nearby and the stillness overwhelmed him. Patrick lay on the dirt floor and counted the days. He had been gone from his home for exactly one week.

He hoped his mother and father were safe. They must be overwhelmed with worry, and he envisioned his mother's tears.

Shivering, he compared the inadequate hut to his British villa. He recalled the spacious sitting room his mother took so much pride in. Smooth wooden benches lined an elaborate table, which was often covered with bowls of fruit and carafes of wine. His throat swelled as a sob from deep within him begged for release. He swallowed it back with the discipline of a soldier.

The weariness of the past week engulfed him, and he tucked the blanket around him and slept.

CHAPTER 11

Brigid

Father began to teach me druid rites while we waited for Maithghean to approve me for formal training. I'd already been learning plant identification and uses with Elían for years. But Maithghean took his time to announce my acceptance.

I learned anyway. Some days Father and I would focus on rituals. He'd practice with me incantations, the movements, and parts of the physical magic: how animal sacrifices should be added to a fire, the prophecies of their entrails. Some things remained sacred, and he refused to show me until I was formally part of the druid order. Other days, we'd turn our attention to an aspect of nature. The most important skill was to observe. I studied the earth, sky, storms, and sun.

"What patterns do you see, Brigid? Are there omens for the harvest?"

I glanced upward. White fluffy clouds filled the sky, things that dictated our agricultural lives.

"They should have two dry days, enough to cut the last of the oats into shocks." I held up one finger and tested the direction of the wind. "I think in three or four days, we will have more rain. Cold rain. Samhain is near."

Father seemed impressed with my weather predictions, which I found simple to make. The closing of our season with the Samhain ceremony was always cold, a reminder of the spirits passing through on those nights. And we lived in Éire. Rain was an easy prediction.

"What names do we use for the Goddess in ritual before a battle?" Father asked, changing the lesson to bards and storytelling.

"Macha," I answered promptly.

He reached for my necklace, tied with a leather cord around my neck. I had worn it since my birth, a gift from him. It was simple copper, forged to form three adjoining spirals.

"What does this mean?" he asked.

"It's the cycle of birth and rebirth. These are never ending, as is the spiral." I pulled it back from his hand. The talisman dangled on its heavy leather thong between my fingertips.

"That is a partial meaning," he said. "The three spirals also represent three goddesses. There are three others, not just Macha. What are their names?" Father waited for my answer to an easy child's question. They were the names I called out in my sleep.

"Other goddesses of this island are Banba, Fodla, and, of course, Eiru, after whom this island was named."

"Eiru was one of the Danann, the children of Danu. Of course, you know what most common people believe about the Danann?" Why was he asking me children's questions? Father kept a steady gaze on me. "Most people believe that the Danann mysteriously turned into the Little Folk, like fairies. Father's tone turned severe, much as Maithghean's did. "You had nightmares as a child. You still do."

Father waited for a response from me, and I refused to give him one. I would not share the Danann dreams. Until I understood what they meant, I would not speak of them to Father or to Maithghean. I would observe, as I was being taught to do, and study the patterns shown to me in the night.

"Our stories remind the tribe of the Danann mysteries," Father continued his lesson.

"Don't people need to remember the Danann as they were?" I asked. "People want gods who are powerful, not hiding under the rocks like na daoine sí. We shouldn't think of them as fairy folk any longer." The words flowed through me unbidden. I clutched the rock beneath me to steady my shaking hands. I had dreamed of them the night before. Swords. Blood Battle. *Save us!* They cried. And the same pulling at me, clutching at me, dragging me down with them. The amber-eyed man who wouldn't set me free. I woke up screaming and breathless.

"We remember many of the Danann as powerful gods, such as Lugh," Father continued. "We celebrate his gift of the sun each season. And, of course, during Imbolc we remember your namesake, Brigid, the goddess of Imbolc, of lament, of healing, do we not?"

I gasped with a sudden jolt, a vision that flashed before me and it was me. *Brigid...lambs...lament...immense sorrow, immense fear.* I saw her, yet I was her. Voices and images filled my mind, jumbled into an incomprehensible pattern. It was a vision, but it was also a memory. Even stronger was the feeling that I should not tell anyone, that I needed first to remember for myself.

CHAPTER 12

Patrick

E scape should have been easy. Alone on the green, rocky hills day in and day out, Patrick was often lonely and mostly bored. Weeks passed. His job as a shepherd was to let the sheep out to pasture and make sure they stayed within the proper borders.

They kidnapped me for this? He often wondered to himself. What would happen if he let the sheep into the next pasture? Probably be beaten...he'd seen the bruises on Maura's face. Eamon and Conall both had scars, though Patrick didn't ask from what. He never did allow the animals outside their borders, guided instead by some innate sense of responsibility.

Every morning, Patrick let the sheep out of their pen, as Liam had shown him. He followed the sheep, studying them. Lambs stayed close to their ewes, who were very protective of their young. They all seemed healthy to him, but he wasn't sure what a sick sheep looked like. Would he be punished if the animal were sick? What should he do if it was? No one answered his questions. When he wasn't worrying about the sheep, he planned his return to Britannia.

After the animals meandered away, he stood on the hillside, unsure of what to do. There were no tutors telling him to study verb conjugation nor soldiers making him practice drills and formations. He was cold and hungry, yet a temporary thrill of freedom sped through him. If I'm here alone, he thought, I should be able to escape. Rapidly, he began organizing his thoughts toward that goal.

Patrick spent the morning exploring his surroundings without letting the sheep out of his sight. He climbed the hills, searching for the sea, any hint of direction that could lead him back home to Britannia. A rumble from his stomach reminded him that his pasty mix of oats and grains were not enough. *If I'm going to eat, I need to hunt. And if I'm going to escape, I need to store a supply of food.*

Thick woodlands bordered the cleared pasturelands of grass, and he ran to the edge, hesitating as he reached the shadowy stands of alder and oak. *Weapons,* he thought as he spied fallen branches. He began to collect an armful of stout wood and paused. *I have no knife.* He grasped the low limb of a sturdy oak. *No sharp tool to carve a point.* Patrick closed his eyes as tears threatened and stung.

A sound of trickling water roused him. Thirst motivated him more than his hunger. Taking a cautious step into the forest, he found a small stream winding through the trees and darting back out toward the pasture. Gratefully, he lapped up the clear liquid. Then he saw a splash. And then another. *Fish.* He looked closely and saw a surfeit of salmon. He reached into the stream, expecting to catch the salmon in his hand. The creatures slithered past.

He picked up one of the branches, stabbing it into the water, missing the fish that slid beneath. In hope of finding any kind of tool, he ran back to his hut, rummaging through his small pile of belongings. He had no metal for a hook, no twine or thread to dangle. He returned to the stream and watched the salmon swim swiftly in the clear water. He grabbed at them with both hands and succeeded in splashing cold water on his only tunic.

"Patience," he said aloud, in Latin. "Help me, dear Lord, to catch this fish." He recalled his soldier's instruction. But even in their survival training, they were given supplies. He was determined to catch a fish. He took a deep breath, said a quick prayer for calm, and let his hands dangle over the bank. The salmon glided past, and his stomach growled in anticipation. He had plans for this first fish: broiled over the small fire in his hut. Patrick thought if he caught more than one, he could cook several at once and begin to stockpile food. He closed his hand around the next fish that tickled his fingertips, but it was too quick.

He lay on his stomach, hands icy and wrinkled, as the sun began to set. He groaned and turned onto his back. A distant *baa* jolted him upright. *The sheep! Where were they?* Patrick ran down the hillside and stopped short. The simple animals had gathered at the bottom of the hill, searching for a new patch of grass.

Patrick climbed back to the bank of the stream, determined, and stuck his hand into the frigid waters again. The fish swam past, through his fingers, around his palms. Any movement scared them off. One finally stilled and Patrick moved fast. He scooped the fish out of the water and threw it on the grass. He was jubilant. He would eat.

"I caught one! I did it! Maith thú!" A few of the ewes rose from their resting places, wary of the noise. Patrick hopped from one foot to the next, yelling to the sky, the land, and to the sheep. No one heard that his cries of joy were in Irish.

CHAPTER 13

Brigid

I began my formal apprenticeship to Elían the healer when Maithghean finally gave his permission. He took the entire winter to mull over the idea. "He's doing it to torture us, just a little," Mother said. "He knows perfectly well Brigid has the druid talent."

Father defended him. "It's not just about accepting her. He needs to decide which path would be best and what places are available. She may be a healer or a bard or a seer."

Mother shook her head. "She's been following Elían since she could walk. Maithghean knows this."

When the Sena discovered my admittance as an acolyte to the druid order, she paid a visit to our house and demanded that Bacene begin his studies as well.

"He is your son, Dubhtach!" She was breathless from the walk to our farm. Bacene stood at her side, his breeches dirty from rough play. Mother slipped out to the stables, unwilling to be in the same room as Sena.

"I realize that, Sena," my father said. "How could I train him when you kept him from me for years? Now you want him alongside me? You should have considered his future in the midst of your selfishness."

Her skin turned pink, a delicate shadow from her cheeks all the way to the roots of her fair hair. Bacene stuck his tongue out at me, a supremely juvenile gesture, considering he was nearly a young man and applying for druid apprenticeship. I ignored him as I continued to study the quartz crystals on the table in front of me. I had struck them against the flint and created a spark, a trick I mastered long ago.

Now, I searched internally for the source of the flame. Bacene sat himself down across from me, apparently bored with his parents' conversation.

"What talent has he shown?" Father asked. "I haven't seen any interest in prophecy work from him, nothing in the way of the healing arts."

I stiffened. The healer's path was mine, not Bacene's.

"Bacene is an excellent storyteller. He has the makings of a bard!"

Of course he's an excellent storyteller, I thought spitefully. He lies all the time.

"It takes more than just telling stories," said Father. "He must learn the entire tribe's stories, our history, the history of each family and each warrior."

"Bacene knows the rigors of druid study. He's learned my lineage and yours and can recite them perfectly."

"Do you? Do you know your own heritage?" Father sat down next to his son, who stared at him with what I saw as a mix of hatred and love. Bacene turned briefly to Sena as if torn. He'd been taught to hate Father and now he must show him respect.

"Some of it," he whispered. He acted like a child just to tug at Father's heart-strings. I slammed the quartz and flint together, producing another wisp of smoke. Father's attention remained on his son.

"Tell me what you know," Father encouraged. "Go on. Start with yourself and go from there."

Bacene recited his own genealogy. As he spoke, I thought of the words along with him. Without trying, I knew the history of our family. He began with Sena and Dubhtach and continued on to their parents before them and those before them. He named their clan leaders and battle heroes. I had to admit his knowledge impressed me and I focused on Bacene, rather than wondering how I knew the genealogy without being taught. I was sure Sena had forced him to memorize for weeks, but the agony paid off. Father, too, was impressed by his son's recitations.

"You may have the makings of a fine bard. I will speak to the order tomorrow."

By Law, our house must remain open to visitors, and we had many. Father's reputation and hospitality was well known throughout the land, and more travelers chose to stay with us instead of Maithghean. Traveling bards, healers, and traders brought us news from the rest of Éire.

"Our head druid is too involved with the chieftain," one healer named Conor complained as he sat with father in front of the hearth. He had been sent to gather particular medicinal herbs from our territory, unable to find the plant in his land. I had accompanied him and Elían on their foraging mission earlier, but had been forbidden to speak. I was in training and my task was to observe, not to interrupt our visitor with questions. Any healing questions I had about the plants and their properties would be reserved for Elían at the proper time.

Conor spoke honestly to Father about his tribe's leadership because he trusted my father completely. Druids knew Father would keep their words in confidence. "We don't know if his interpretations of the throwing sticks are true or said for the gain of the clan chieftain." From my spying on the sacred grove, I knew Maithghean would like my father to make a few readings in the same way. He also pushed for battle, for any choice that would expand Dunlang's land holdings beyond our borders and increase our numbers of valuable cattle.

Conor continued with his complaints. He'd had several pints of ale with his supper, making him loose-tongued. "Corruption like this is the reason why a few from my village have turned to the Roman god." Conor gulped his brew.

"The Roman gods?" asked Father. "Rome is far over the sea. Why would anyone here have an interest in their beliefs?"

"There have been visitors to our land, and some of them teach about their one god."

"One?" Father asked. "I heard of this, years ago, but left it to rumors."

"Certainly you've heard of Palladius? He visited during our father's time. Being so close to a harbor, I suppose we are the first to meet these visitors. Palladius spoke highly of his faith," Conor said. "But I remember my father..." He smiled as he recalled his tale. "My father laughed in his face. He told Palladius that the Irish wouldn't abandon their traditions. Sent him on his way."

I sat quietly beside Father, struggling to keep my silence. Conor occasionally nodded in my direction in recognition of my acolyte status. Mother stayed at the table, carding wool.

"Should we be worried? After all, Palladius has been gone for years with no apparent influence." Father didn't sound very concerned.

"That group, begun by Palladius, lives in stone huts along the strand. An odd practice," Conor took another gulp of ale. "We host Christian visitors, now and then. Travelers, freed slaves looking for others who share their beliefs."

"Then what is the problem, if they're so few in number?" said Father.

"There is no slavery in their community," Conor said. "They say their god, Christ, was poor in material things, but rich in spirit. He does not follow the hierarchies. This status, that status, chieftain, druid, warrior, slave. None of that matters to their god."

"No slavery?" Mother rarely interrupted Father's conversations but she'd approached as soon as Conor spoke of Palladius's followers. Conor took note of her gray skirt. He cleared his throat.

"Brocca, bring more ale, please." Father was calm, quiet. But the command was there. I knew Brehon Law. I knew the hierarchy of our social structure. Yet I wished the earth would swallow me. I was embarrassed for my mother, whose mouth was tight with lines as she searched the kitchen for a new crock of cider.

"Now," Father returned to Conor and they faced each other in front of the fire. "This ...random community doesn't seem to be a threat."

"They are a threat," said Conor. "Or they could be, if they continue to grow." He inclined his head toward Mother. "I'm worried. You should be too."

Battle brimmed under the hot summer sun. From the edge of the village, shouts and taunts and ferocious clashes of weapons rang out over Fotharit. Chariots careened over the hillside as men made their way to the battlefields. Summer was the time of cattle raids—either raid or be raided.

"Men of Fotharit!" Dunlang thrust his sword into the air, and his warriors gathered around him. "Let us protect our people and protect our land!" The neighboring tribe of Uí Neíll had stolen two-dozen of our cows and caused the death of three good warriors, an enormous cost. Without the cows, we were impoverished. Without our warriors, we were vulnerable. With a wild yell, the warriors thundered into the distance.

Father accompanied the warriors, casting his predictions for their outcome. Tagdh , no longer an acolyte, sang the songs of heroes as they marched to war.

The entire village had gathered in the morning to see them off, and it seemed like a festival-day. I shivered in anticipation as I watched the scene of warriors and druids. Mother and I walked home behind the dusty caravan of chariots and foot soldiers, and they crashed past our house toward the road north, toward the enemy tribe.

"Go inside, Brigid," she said as I lingered in the doorway.

"I want to watch the warriors return," I begged. The racing horses and flashing swords excited me. One day, I would be a healer and would heal the warriors' wounds. Father would not let me accompany Elían to the battlefield. "There will be enough time for your training when we return."

"They just left," Mother chided. "Besides, you won't be so excited about their return. It's a bloody sight, full of death and sadness." Mother pulled me indoors as the dust from the chariots settled.

"I've seen wounds before. And now, I can help them," I said. "Elían has shown me how to bandage surface injuries. And today, I'll learn even more."

Determined to act as if it were a normal day, Mother began her chores, yet opened the front door after each task, checking for Father.

We kept busy. We organized the flour sacks and filled covered pots with wheat. We aired out the bedding. As I shook out each blanket, as I swept the floor, I played a child's game to convince myself. If I swept the earthen floor faster, then our side would win. If I churned the butter before noon sun, the warriors would return safely. If I gathered the sheep from the pasture, Elían would allow me to help with battle mending. I'd worked with her on emergency care around the tuath, bandaging minor cooking burns or pulling stitches from a warrior's wound. But, I'd yet to be part of a major battle. This time, I was certain Elían would need my help.

At sunset, the triumphant warriors of Fotharit returned home. Chariots rumbled past our house. A parade of victors entered the village. Trophy heads, with bloody neck stumps and eyes frozen in fear, hung from chariot rims of winning warriors. The dead stared at me as they passed.

Maithghean and Father reached our house and left the caravan of warriors and cattle. My father looked tired and disheveled, while Maithghean's eyes snapped, energized by the raid. The line above my mother's brow relaxed as the two men went inside, gulping pitchers of water and ale to quench their thirst.

The injured and dead bodies passed next on a convoy of bloody wagons. I searched for Elían. Men, gashed by swords, limbs missing, cried for their mothers. Women ran out to meet their slain husbands and sons. Wails of loss sent chills of revulsion down my back.

Maithghean grabbed my shoulders and bent to whisper in my ear. "You want to be a healer, Brigid? This is what you must see." I shuddered at his touch, almost as revolting as the injuries I had witnessed. He reached inside me again, pulling at my energy, my power. He tried again and again to take it from me. Just as we gather energy from the earth during rituals, he tried to gather mine and take it for himself.

"Stop it!" I twisted out of his grasp, my mouth dry.

"Can you accept blood and death, young Brigid?" His eyes pinned my gaze beneath his. I couldn't answer. My voice, unable to find words, stuck in my throat. "You can heal them. You have the power to heal them all if you try."

Warriors who were uninjured carried the hurt on litters of leather hides between them. They trudged past, and the blank stare of one warrior whose comrades carried him followed me, his innards visible through the massive gash in his gut. I swallowed hard, thinking he must be dead.

"He's not dead," Maithghean whispered into my ear. "He will live for hours, even days, with his intestines shown for all to see. Stomach injuries are a slow, painful wound."

The man's eyes widened when he saw Maithghean. He reached a feeble hand toward the magician.

"Yes, I will tend to you," Maithghean spoke to the dying warrior and then continued his whispered conversation to me. "Entrails make a powerful portend."

"No!" This time Maithghean pushed me back, away from the warrior..

"You must remember, Brigid, how it is to tend to wounded warriors, don't you? So many sons lost to the sword. Brigid of the Danann, bringer of laments."

I backed away from him, unable to speak, into the house.

Mother handed me a stack of linen rags. Her words broke the spell that kept me silenced. "Take these to Elían. She will need your help." She turned her attention to my father, forgetting that Maithghean lurked outside our door.

I ran from Maithghean to the field of injured men instead. I was overwhelmed, no longer by sickness, but by sadness. These men were dying and already the scent of putrefied wounds wafted in the breeze. They cried and begged to be put out of their pain.

"Please, girl." One man grabbed my ankle as I passed. I gasped in surprise, stumbling to my knees. "Bring me hemlock. Send me to my next life, may it be better than this!"

What could I do, a young girl sent on an errand by my mother? His grasp went limp, and I ran to find Elían, my ankle red with his blood.

CHAPTER 14

Patrick

Alone, he wandered through the hills, searching for paths, ways to leave. From his perch on the high hill, he saw the western sea glinting in the sunlight. The vast ocean was one border of his prison. His aim was to go east and follow the coast until he came to a harbor. Although he could see the ocean to the west, he saw no ships. Ships would take him home. The harbor where he was bought, unconscious, was at least a day's journey by wagon away, and a single track led north. Perhaps he should veer north and east, toward Rathlin. But that was where Seamus lived. He had no desire to run into the burly pirate again. Straight east it would be.

One mid-summer night, he decided it was time. Once the harvest began, he would be confined to the slave quarters on Milliuc's farm for the winter, surrounded by other people, rendering any chance of leaving impossible. He couldn't fathom sleeping in that hovel with all those people. Patrick hadn't forgotten his life of privilege. He might be a slave and a shepherd, but at least this falling down hut was his.

He reviewed his cache of provisions. He saved every scrap of bread he could manage and dried salmon from the stream. Along with the fish, he picked what greens he knew, including wild mustard and spring onions.

With scraps of leather from his tattered breeches, Patrick cut strips for a sling with the sharpest rock he could find. It was a crude weapon, and when he practiced with it, he only skimmed the sides of two rabbits. He wished for tools, a blade, to carve sapling branches for a decent bow and arrow. He needed to be much closer to his target if the slingshot were to work.

His torn wool blanket became a knapsack. He tossed in his supply of food and tied the top of the bulk into a knot. There was no other way for him to carry his provisions, and he wouldn't leave the blanket behind. At night, he would need it for warmth. The tunic he had worn since leaving Britannia was little more than rags. More importantly, he knew he could survive. He had to. His confidence would make up for the lack of clothing.

He had at least a week's worth of dried salmon and his water bag was full. Still, he worried. What if he didn't find a stream? What if he ran out of water? Rain pattered softly on his roof. Dying of thirst would be difficult in Éire. He'd leave tonight. Milliuc or his farmhands would spot him too easily during the day.

The moon was full and it would light his way. He stepped outside of his hut, exhilarated, his supplies slung over his bony shoulder.

"Deo juvante." He sent his prayer in Latin, a way to celebrate his journey home. He tucked his sling into his pocket, just in case predators drew near. The sheep dotted the nighttime landscape; ewes and lambs curled together. He bid the animals farewell with a wave of his hand.

He walked with lightness in his step. Stones no longer bruised his feet, which were now tough as leather. It was silent except for the occasional bleat of a lamb, and a faint breeze danced from hilltop to mound. How shocked his parents will be when they see him. He was like one of the Gaulish folk, bearded and hair below his ears. That wouldn't do for a decuriones's son at all, Patrick imagined his father saying. He couldn't be trusted with the citizens' tax money. The city council would be ashamed.

East, toward the sunrise. A distant howl of a wolf caused the hairs on the back of his neck to rise, and he touched the sling in his pocket for reassurance.

Before the sun rose, he began a steep descent. Easy. Then, he promptly twisted his ankle on the rocky slope. Not so easy. He picked his way carefully through the rocks. Be careful.

As the pink rays of morning light approached, Patrick found himself outside a ring fort, surprised at how simple it was. He had seen glimpses of the stone-encircled fort from his vantage on the forested hilltop, but hadn't realized it was so close. Perhaps too close. He wondered if Milliuc traded his goods here.

Smoke drifted upward from the hearth fires of round thatched homes within the enclosure. Clanging sounds rang through the air as the village smith began his work for the day. Patrick's stomach growled when he smelled roasting meat—venison, he guessed. He rested on the outskirts, finding shelter under three boulders, stacked like a bridge.

Two peasant girls from an outlying farm walked by, carrying earthen jugs for water. He remained in his hiding place under the dolmen. Most likely, the girls were neighbors of Milliuc, and he couldn't risk being seen.

"Bless the spirits, in their rest," the girls whispered as they passed. Spirits? He remembered Liam's warning of na daoine sí. He crouched under the lintel of the stones and saw behind him a dark opening. He wouldn't be scared by some silly talk of fairies beneath the stones.

Patrick reckoned he had been gone from Britannia for three months or so, judging as he could by the moon cycles. He had survived on minimal food and water, in addition to desolation on the hillside with flocks of sheep; a far cry from his mornings in the villa, rich breakfasts of eggs, bread, and meat brought to him by servants.

The peasant girls passed by again, their chore, filling their containers with water at the spring, completed. Patrick thought of Lupida and Darceca and young Darys. He wondered how they were and hoped, at the very least, they were kindly treated. Overall, for himself, he knew he had fared well under the circumstances.

He ran to the spring with his water bag and filled it, wishing he had a proper basket or satchel to carry his things. Maybe he should go back to the village and barter. He had nothing to trade, though, and the locals might know by now that Milliuc was looking for his shepherd boy.

Patrick threw his makeshift bag over his shoulder again and decided to get as far from the fort as possible. If bartering for goods became necessary, it would have to be farther away from Milliuc's tribal land. Abruptly, his bundle spilled. Patrick stooped to gather the pieces of dried salmon when rough hands seized him.

"What... ?" A meaty fist slammed into his mouth. His head rang and his face pulsed from the blow. Blood sprayed from his lips. A second assailant held his arms behind his back while the first took direct aim at his stomach. Patrick gasped for air, afraid he was going to be sick. He struggled against the man holding his arms.

"Milliuc's been looking for you," the first man sneered. Patrick focused on a burly, stocky warrior whose right arm was the size of Patrick's own thigh. His efforts to escape had been in vain. He strained his bony teenaged arms, but the warrior's grip held him firm. Another flash of pain crossed his face, and he heard a resonating thump. That's me on the ground, he thought ridiculously, and then he thought no more.

CHAPTER 15

The waters of the bay faded from view as we began the long walk south in the warmth of late spring. The druids journeyed to the sacred hill of Druin Criadh to bless the land before another battle. The earlier raid gave Dunlang, encouraged by Maithghean, enough confidence to try another. We followed behind the warriors and offered prayers and rituals as they sped ahead in their chariots.

The landscape shifted from the tidewater plains of my childhood to rounded hills and purple mountains. Mists shrouded the mountain ridge. Thin golden light filtered between the curves of the foothills.

The time had come for battle instruction. As students, Bacene and I would observe life and death to understand the life cycle completed in war. Druids blessed the warriors. Bards sang the songs of heroes to intimidate the enemy. I focused on my healer's preparation with Elían. Bacene would walk onto the battlefield and play his bodhran for the fallen. He'd memorize their names, their family histories, the feats they accomplished in battle.

Another reason for the journey was to visit the sacred oak, an ancient tree that grew on the borderland between tribes. No one tribe could claim it; no one ever harmed it. Druids from all over Éire gathered at the oak for rare ceremonies. The tree stood alone on the empty plain. Its roots, hundreds of years old, wound down beneath the hill. It was my first visit to the sacred oak.

"I want to be on the battlefield just as Bacene will," I argued with my father as we traveled. "If I'm to be a healer, then I need to get to the warriors as soon as possible."

"No, Brigid. You have no place there yet."

"But my grandmother was a clan chieftain. She fought in battles."

"She was also a Pict." His slur on my mother's creed didn't go unnoticed. No wonder Mother waited for more news about the communities Conor had described. She'd found a messenger willing to travel for bits of gold she gave him. Father didn't know. She wanted to find the people who lived without slaves, without druids, without the Law.

Father continued. "You are a healer, not a warrior. You'll go when Elían allows and only then."

Energy gathered in my brow, and I put my hand to my forehead, willing the heat to cool.

"We'll discuss the history and art of war before the battle begins," he conceded. "Will that settle your curiosity? Then, you'll prepare for the wounded with Elían."

We had reached the sacred oak. Its power was immense and energy radiated from it. Wisdom had been stored in it for generations. Its thirsty roots had absorbed all the knowledge from all the tribes of the land.

Warriors camped along the ridgeline, where they organized their weapons and practiced sword thrusts, away from the tree. Generations of thick roots tangled like solid veins. The druids gathered beneath the tree, its trunk so wide that five men could encircle it with their arms outstretched. We found places to stand within the knotted roots. Maithghean led the druids in an ancient ritual that acknowledged the power we all felt. His hands rose and grasped as if he clutched the energy. We followed his motions, hands raised. It was true; the power could be grasped. It wound its way through me, and I felt the strength that ran deep into the ground. I pulled it up from the ground, as water would flow through the tree, storing it. The force of this oak had protected tribes since the beginning of the island. The deep-rooted power ran through me, something old and unnamed.

We joined hands, all the druids, even Bacene, to honor what was true.

The ritual ended and we stayed in our circle, waiting for the hum of the earth and roots to dissipate.

"This is what we must bring to our warriors tomorrow," said Maithghean. "They will need to take this energy and strength with them into battle. Save it, use it."

When the druids left, Father began his lesson as promised. "What do warriors do with their trophies once they return home?"

"They dedicate them to Macha." I had seen my father preside over many of those rites that honored the dead enemies who sacrificed their lives. I recalled the trophy heads that hung from the sides of the warriors' chariots. Was that Macha's wish or the warriors?

"Has Macha always been a goddess of war?" he asked.

"No, she was originally a creator. She was one of the first on this land." I replied to his question by rote. Macha filled my dreams, especially during my childhood. Now her presence returned to me in full force. A vision. Druids had them - some druids. I let the sight fill me. I walked on the battle plain, translucent, filled with light, with hair as bright as the sun. She walked with Dagda, a large, robust man, yet he was as translucent as she. They reached for me through grassy fields, more verdant than any I had ever seen. *If we die, so do you. We are all connected together. Save us!*

"Brigid, are you well?" Father asked.

I shook my head, unable to form words. Father clasped my hand, breaking the vision. His grip kept me from returning to that other place. Dizziness overwhelmed me, and the landscape wavered before my eyes. "What do you see? Tell me."

Where did they go? Macha and Dagda had been walking toward me. I was ready to greet them when Father broke the spell. Feelings of sadness, longing crashed through me, as if I knew them and our reunion interrupted. I didn't answer Father. My childhood intuition to keep quiet about the Danann surfaced again. *Don't tell him about the vision.*

"Brigid? What did you see?" He handed me a water bag. I would not speak of what I saw. Father's concern stayed with me. "We're done with the talk of the Old Ones for today. Can you stand? Go to Elfan and help with the medicinal preparations. You'll not set foot on the battlefield until the fighting has ended. Whatever vision you've had will be doubly dangerous. Do you hear?"

"Yes, Father." My head pounded and the earth swirled around me. I didn't think I'd be able to set foot on the battlefield.

Tens of warriors lined the field. Sunlight gleamed off pointed swords and copper breastplates. The warriors of both tribes had decorated their hair with lime. The paste caused their normally flowing manes to stand on end, giving them the appearance of crazed monsters ready to kill.

I helped Elían prepare remedies for the incoming wounded. She would take bandages and medicines onto the field while I stayed behind to cut linen for bandages and grind herbs with the mortar and pestle. It's not fair, I thought impetuously, now that my vision sickness had worn off. A druid should be trained in all aspects of healing. I should be on the field as well, dressing bandages, providing relief to the wounded. My upset wasn't really due to the rules Elían set forth; I was jealous that Bacene would follow Tagdh and learn songs for the deceased. As I walked toward Elían's tent with a supply of bandages, I noticed that a faint deer trail led to a stand of boulders ten men's lengths from the site of combat. The stones tempted me. How easy it would be to hide. The warriors wouldn't notice me.

They met in the field's center, deciding whether to fight between champions or engage in full battle. Both sides taunted each other, hurling insults about their champion. They waved their weapons to show who had the better sword, the sharpest arrows. The jeers and calls to the enemy echoed across the land.

Two paths angled before me. I hesitated. I started toward the campsite where Elían expected me to go. She would need the bandages. I admitted to myself that my assigned job wasn't useless. But, I stopped at the path's fork and turned toward the stones. The immovable stone called to me. I would stay long enough to see which method of fighting the warriors chose. That's all. Then, I would continue to the healer's tent. After all, if they chose a single champion, my work would be over quickly and I kept several powders in the pouch at my belt. I scrambled through the boulders, vying for both the best vantage point and hiding spot. Two stones formed a V, and I crouched into the inside space.

Dunlang called from his chariot. "Who do you offer as your champion?"

"Broen is our champion!" was the reply from across the field.

The men of Fotharit shouted belittling remarks about Broen's fighting skills. Dunlang stood tall in his chariot, despite the jeers, and debated the choice set before him. Broen was an esteemed fighter. Their bards sang praises of his feats and of his beheading a man in one stroke. The shouted taunts wouldn't change what their chieftain knew to be true. There wasn't a single fighter to match him. The best chance from Fotharit was Lugaid; he'd been chosen before, and stood proud and waiting. But he had never killed a man in a single stroke. His well-known endurance, a supernatural ability to fight for hours, was his gift. Dunlang surveyed the army of the enemy. I sensed his thoughts; Fotharit would win in battle, not with a single champion.

The stones were a perfect shelter as I watched. No one noticed me, wedged into the small space. My blood tingled and a shiver went down my spine, although the summer day was warm. I leaned into the stones and felt the pull of the Earth's energy. *You know us,* the boulders seemed to say. *We will protect you.*

"I ask for your champion!" Broen's voice thundered across the field and reverberated on the shield of every warrior.

Lugaid stepped forward, unable to refuse the request but Dunlang called, "We haven't agreed to single combat. Your impulsiveness doesn't bode well for your clan."

A sinking feeling overwhelmed me. The vision returned. I melded deeper into the granite. *You are bound to us,* Dagda said. *Remember* I pushed against the stones but they held me. I needed to go to Elían before a full battle was chosen.

Why does the stone bind me?

You are one of us.

Macha. I knew her. She spoke to me in my mind as if she were next to me.

Shouts broke through my semi-conscious state. I struggled to understand the vision. Chariot wheels thundered. Dunlang had refused single combat, and I was still on this battlefield.

In times of life and death, men turned to their animal instinct to survive. Their growls and hisses sheltered their minds from the natural aberration of killing one of their own. Each thought they were the hunters. Both were hunted. Swords clanged in the air. Loud crashes of metal assaulted my senses. I was horrified at what I had been so eager to see. I could have touched a brown haired man who fell before me. Not a man, a boy—he had no mustache. Only light fuzz had formed on his upper lip. Blood droplets hung there, dripping from the wound to his eye.

Uncontrolled trembling permeated my body. I didn't know if it was from the current battle or from the vision. I began to reach for the warrior, with my instinct to heal, and then stopped. I sensed Maithghean's presence nearby, causing a prickling on the back of my neck.

Bacene and Tagdh appeared with the druids to sing for the fallen boy. The bards called to the spirit world for the hero who had passed. They sang his family history, committing it to memory again. The boy had followed his father into battle, continuing the lineage of warriors, and now that lineage ended. Bacene's voice carried, strong and sure, with a steady beat on his bodhran.

Fighting continued. Men fell, oozing intestines and blood. Blood drenched the green grass, giving a rusted stain among the chaos, screaming, and confusion. Men writhed in pain and triumph.

Dimly, awareness came to me. *Brigid.* Maithghean's voice. *Help our chieftain. You have the power to reach him.*

How could he be inside my head? How does he know? *Brigid, use your powers! Use them!* The voices from the vision.

With a sense of unreality, I focused on Dunlang. A warrior had crept behind the chieftain's chariot, ready to strike.

Behind you!

Dunlang turned and thrust his sword deep into the warrior's heart. The man wilted on the steps of the chieftain's chariot, the look of surprise on his face. Fotharit had won. The warriors returned to camp, slow, tired, but victorious. Slain bodies littered the field, and the druids stood among them, blessing the dead and treating the injured. I must tend to them, I thought. I'm the healer. Maithghean's eyes cut a path across the field, finding mine.

CHAPTER 16

Patrick

The patter of rain woke Patrick. The light was an indeterminate shade of gray, and he couldn't tell if it was dawn or dusk. Pain coursed through him. His stomach ached from the repeated blows. His eyes were dry and crusted with blood. Lying on his side, he saw a shimmering in the far corner. The air seemed to quiver.

"Bí láidir."

Patrick rested his forehead on the damp ground again. He must have been struck on the back of the head. He was hearing things.

"Be strong," the voice said again. Patrick sat up and moaned as his body protested the movement. The room spun again and he swallowed several times to calm his nauseous stomach. He tried to focus the blur in front of his eyes.

"What? What's going on?"

"You're speaking in Irish. Did you notice?"

Patrick started to speak, but then stopped himself. Dathi? Why was Dathi the druid in his hut? He stood shakily, which only led to more lightheadedness. It was dark now and rain fell in a steady beat. How long had he been asleep? He opened the door, and a rush of dampness kept him from fainting. He let the rain soak his face, washing the dried blood from his mouth and nose.

Chilled, he returned indoors and sank to the floor in exhaustion. The druid sat on the far side - as far as it could be in the hut - and had built a fire. Hungry and tired, Patrick believed his feeble mind played tricks on him. He reached for his water bag and held it under the doorway to collect rainwater.

"Why are you here?" he asked, not sure if the man was real.

"Irish again." Dathi said. "You'll remember soon enough." He pushed a loaf of bread and a basket of apples toward him. At the bottom of the basket was a folded blanket.

Patrick had spoken in Irish. How did he know the language? For the thousandth time since the raider's ship, he contemplated how he gained the knowledge. No, he'd be able to recall some piece of a tutoring lesson. He wrapped the blanket around himself and chewed on a chunk of bread. He knew Irish on Seamus's boat. How?

Dathi watched him saying nothing. If he had been in less pain, Patrick might have been terrified of the bald druid in his hut. But at the moment he was exhausted. Confused. And exhausted. He took a long quaff of water and slumped into sleep again against the straw.

Maura's boys, Nial and Liam, climbed the slopes to the pasture. They eyed Patrick's purplish face dubiously.

"This is for you." Nial, a thin, pale boy, dropped a bundle at Patrick's feet. Food. He'd finished the bread Dathi had brought days ago. He grabbed at the cheese and fresh bread like an animal, causing the boys to step back. They watched as he tore into the great chunks of brown bread, ignoring the pain of his bruised lips.

"We let the sheep out. They shouldn't be penned up like that for so long," Liam said. Patrick glared at him, but continued to stuff his bruised mouth full of food.

"Am I in trouble?" he asked after he'd finished the loaf.

"Looks like you've already been punished," said Liam. "Besides, you can't go anywhere. People will keep watch for you."

He wanted to ask more questions but remembered he wasn't supposed to know the language too well. He grabbed at the cheese, biting into the thick wheel. He could tell Nial and Liam were waiting, perhaps for a piece themselves, but Patrick shook his head. He was starving and wasn't in the mood to share. The boys left, unrewarded for their labors.

So, Milliuc wasn't going to punish him further. Patrick went inside and lay down again, his head aching. Somewhere, his guards would always be on the lookout. Patrick was a prisoner in a wide-open field.

He poked at the embers in his fire circle with a stick. If he could get the fire ablaze, he could figure out Dathi's interest in him. And the language. None of this made sense. The guard's beating must have injured him and now he's seeing things, hearing things.

Patrick rubbed his eyes and took another drink of water, but not before he wished for the ale he and Linus had been drinking when he was kidnapped. He added a few pieces of kindling and had a small but steady fire. He was definitely alone in his hut. He opened the door. No one there. He went outside and let the sheep out of the pen. They'd graze here for a few more days before Milliuc would have them move on to the next pasture.

The fresh air was good for him. He breathed in the green damp. It was good to leave the hut. An injury, he told himself. He had a soft spot on his brain. Soon, it would be sunrise and he'd follow the flock. Maybe he'd try for more salmon from the stream.

He recalled with an uneasy fear how he suddenly knew Irish. Patrick glanced around for another person, some other being. Only the sheep and rolling hills. I never had Irish lessons. Latin, Welsh, a little Greek. The last thing I was doing before all of this was drinking ale and rolling dice with my friend. And now...

Dathi found him again on the hillside. He was startled when the robed druid seemed to appear out of nowhere.

"Why are you here?" Patrick asked. "How are you here?"

"The fort is just beyond that ridge." He pointed vaguely in the direction of a hillside. Patrick thought he had wandered farther than that with the flock. "I'll walk with you before you stray too far." Dathi still made him uneasy but his other option was solitude and the sheep. "And I'll tell you some stories. They may help you."

"Help with what? Unless your stories help me return home, I don't care. There's nothing on this island but barbarians. Feral fiends who kidnapped innocent Britons."

"I'm sorry about that," said Dathi. "Your kidnapping was a horrible trial. But I believe..." He slowed his steps so that Patrick had to stop and look at him. "I believe you are here for a reason. I haven't figured it out yet, not all of it. But you are connected to this land somehow."

The druid's words made no sense. "My only part in this land is figuring out how to leave it."

"That may happen one day but there is much for you to learn about our people, our past."

"I doubt it." Patrick continued walking. It was time to turn the flock eastward, to a fresh patch of grass.

Now it was Dathi who struggled to keep up with him. "Druids, you see, believe in many lives. We are born into one, live our cycle, then continue into another. The purpose of all our ceremonies is really that. To follow and honor that cycle of birth and rebirth."

Patrick stabbed his oak walking staff into the earth. He'd found the fallen branch a perfect height for him. It was a thick branch that might provide protection if he had to fight Milliuc's guards again.

"Sometimes we meet our friends again, our anam cara, sometimes we meet our rivals."

"Your beliefs sound complicated. For Christians, we die and go to heaven. Or hell." He hadn't thought much about it one way or the other but he felt he had to argue with Dathi.

"I've heard of this. There are occasional wanderers who follow the teachings of a man called Pallidus. He brought to Ireland this simplistic belief."

"There's been a Christian here?"

"Long ago, in my father's time." Dathi shrugged. "Some people seem to like simplicity. That's not you." He held Patrick by the arm, forcing him to stop and look at the eastern view of hills and forest. "From the first time I saw you, I felt it. A knowing."

Patrick nearly burst out laughing. "Trust me, druid, you and I have never known each other. And the sooner I can stop knowing you and get back to Britain, the happier I will be."

Dathi sat on the hillside and motioned Patrick to join him "One day that may happen. Until then, I will tell you stories of our gods. Dagda...Macha...Brigid...do you know any of those names?"

Patrick ignored the faint pang in his middle, the center of his solar plexus, and shook his head.

"I'll tell you about the ancient ones, but just one story for now? This is about the great god called Dagda," said Dathi.

Patrick raised an eyebrow, but listened to the story. There was nothing else to do.

CHAPTER 17

Brigid

B acene and I finished our first level of druid training, and we continued on our paths that would take years to complete, his in bard craft, and mine in healing. Our father's influence, whether in our blood or in his teachings, moved us both ahead quickly. I had worked with Elían, assisting her after battles with basic bandaging and cleansing of wounds. Now, I began to study herbs, potions, and movements of the stars.

Elían and I took long walks in the countryside to identify vegetation. I studied herb lore, the properties held within each plant. The landscape was lush and green in the height of summer, and we walked into the oak forests. We skirted the swampy bogs, gathering what we needed from the edges before the bogs sucked us into their murky depths.

I cherished these walks, away from the tuath , away from the prying eyes of Maithghean. He made no mention of how he commanded me wordlessly to help Dunlang. I spent hours upon our return from Druin Criadh meditating on the strange visions I'd had and how Maithghean spoke in my mind. No answers came to me.

We entered the edges of the forest, stopping near a rowan tree.

"Describe the properties of rowan," Elían said.

I studied the white flowers, which would give way to ripened fruit in a few months. "The bark is used for upset stomachs." I was curious why she gave me an easy question. Rowan bark was a common medicinal in our tuath . "Even making a jelly from the berries helps with digestion."

"In ritual, rowan is powerful. You made a concoction before the battle of Druin Criadh, to give the warriors strength. Do you remember when I first taught you its uses?"

There was so much that I seemed to know without effort. "No, I don't."

"Because I never have." Her eyes narrowed. "You treated the sick children in my care last month after Beltane using a decoction of the rowan branch, to stop their nausea."

It was a simple case of an upset stomach. Several children were queasy following the festival. Likely they all ate the same berries that had gone bad. A line of vomiting children lined up at Elían's door. I had started a batch of the soothing mint medicine before Elían finished examining her first patient.

"It seemed like the right thing to do," I responded.

"It was the right thing to do. I have never used that specific concoction. It's an old method of preparing it, rarely used by healers now. How did you know to prepare it the old way?"

I said nothing. I didn't know. I'd boiled and mixed the herbs intuitively. Seeping, as we did now, would have been a better, stronger potion, but we needed something fast.

Elían sat beneath a large oak and motioned for me to join her. We listened to the rustling of leaves and the scurry of small creatures. Soon, the sounds quieted.

We meditated, drawing strength from the earth. I enjoyed the peacefulness of the exercise, emptying my mind, allowing myself to be in the moment.

"Sometimes," Elían began her lesson. "People are born into this life with memories from their past life. Perhaps this is where your unknown knowledge is from. As a druid, you can draw on your healing power from all your past lives." Elían waited expectantly, her white hair flowing around her in the breeze. "Do you remember, Brigid?" she asked.

I fidgeted, hesitant. The calm peace I'd felt evaporated. Father and Maithghean had asked similar questions when I was young. Now Elían, who I admired as a teacher, asked me the same thing.

"I can't say whether I know things from before," I said. "I don't know."

"What about your dreams?"

"I do have powerful dreams."

She took my hand. Her gray eyes, set within a web of lines and wrinkles, sought mine, urging me to explain. "I've had dreams my whole life." It was dangerous to speak of this, I knew deep inside, yet it was a relief to tell her. "Always the same faces greet me at night. I haven't met them, not now, but it is like I know them as much as I know you, or Mother and Father."

"Do they have names? Do you feel they're your family?"

I hesitated again. *Stop speaking. Stop now.*

"They're family," I faltered. "I have seen a mother and father, sisters, and others." I paused. Why was Elían asking? Why did she want to know? She was my teacher, yes, of plants, herbs, and medicine. Not of the spirit world.

A gust of wind blew through the trees and clouds darkened the sky.

Enough. Say no more.

CHAPTER 18

Patrick

P atrick reviewed Dathi's stories while he was out in the pasture. Since it was
    either that or talk to the sheep, he chose to replay the stories. Old gods, old
founders of the islands, battles, shape-changing. Fanciful stuff.

The flock strayed as far north as they were allowed. A small ring fort was there,
stone walls stacked defensively around the small settlement. Guards stood at the
gate. Dathi had ended his story saying, "We knew you would be able to help
druids."

"I can't help you." Patrick spoke aloud as stared at the guarded fort below. "I
can't help myself." Sodden with rain and defeat, he began to pitch a tent made
of a few branches and woolen tarpaulin woven by Maura. He camped when the
sheep pastured too far from his hut.

"Why me?" he had asked Dathi. "Why not find another druid to tell your stories
to?"

"Because everyone is caught up in battles and raids. We focus on cattle and Law,
not on the gods. There's been something lost and I think you can help the people
reclaim it. You have ... something."

Something. Patrick wrapped a length of wool around his shoulders and tried to
keep dry. He gnawed on a thin strip of dried rabbit meat, having finally managed
to kill a few animals with his makeshift sling. On the ground next to him, a few
twigs fell into the shape of the cross. That was something he knew. That symbol
he understood. He twisted a tuft of wool into a thick string and tied the twigs

together. He pocketed the makeshift cross, thankful for *something* familiar. This is all I have, he thought.

Closing his eyes, he curled up on the spongy ground under his rough lean-to, too tired to argue with his memory of Dathi. His hand clutched the cross of twigs. Patrick drifted off as he recalled Dathi's stories of the people who blended with the earth, with the trees, with the sky. They were part of the land; they were the land until a foreign tribe invaded them. He told him about the sun god, the goddess of wind, the god of mists. He saw the transformations, the story blending with his dreams.

Patrick returned to the farm in late summer to be put to work at the harvest. Milliuc had sent the same two warriors to find him. Patrick hadn't left his land and was irritated at the sight of the guards. Grudgingly, he herded the sheep in their direction and began the walk back.

Harvest was another reason he was taken from the British shores. Threshing the grain crops of oats and wheat required every person's participation. Even though he and Conall and Eamon labored from first light until sundown beating the wheat from its stalk, the grain they stored was hardly enough to last the winter. Wet weather caused mold to spread through much of the stored wheat. Slaughtering cows and sheep for meat added to harvest responsibilities. Patrick couldn't bear to watch Conall and Milliuc slice the throats of the sheep he had tended all summer and was glad to haul heavy loads of oats instead.

He attempted to speak Irish with the others, and pretended that he was learning the language. He dropped a few words here and there, and asked for help with pronunciation.

"You've picked up the language quickly," Milliuc said. He made no further comment when Patrick nodded in agreement.

Living in the crowded quarters was an adjustment. Patrick threw his pile of sleeping rags against a far wall, wedged next to Conall and Eamon. He fought for space between the bulky men and the rough thatch wall, receiving either a kick in the back or a face full of thatched straw in the middle of the night.

"How can Milliuc enslave you? You're all Irishmen." Patrick asked. Maura set out the meal of mutton and brown bread and joined them around a rough-hewn table.

"We were taken as prisoners after our tribe lost a cattle raid," Conall answered, matter of fact. His large fair head shone in the firelight, and his huge hands tore apart the bread. Patrick couldn't imagine anyone taking this bulk of a man as a prisoner. Patrick turned to Eamon, who gestured that his story was the same as Conall's.

"Maura?"

"I was taken from Britannia when I was a child, with my family. I have lived here since."

"So you're British, too!" Patrick was elated. "From where?"

Maura shrugged, and a lock of brown hair streaked with white escaped from its braid. Tiny lines etched the corners of her eyes. Patrick wondered how old she was.

"I don't know. I was only a small child, two or three years old, and the raiders allowed my mother to bring me with her. Took pity on her."

"But you speak Irish. Do you remember any Latin? Or Welsh?"

"No. My mother died from a fever soon after we arrived, and I was separated from the others from my village. I remember very little."

Patrick's shoulders sagged.

Conall broke the uneasy silence that settled over the household. "Do you know her children won't be servants? As the third generation, Liam and Nial, when they come of age, will be full members of the tribe. See, it's not all bad."

"How did you do it?" Conall changed the subject, referring to Patrick's botched escape.

Patrick bowed his head, embarrassed, with his ignorance of hard work and now his inability to escape.

"Come on," Eamon chimed in, his toothy grin too broad in his thin, long face. "Tell us. We've all tried to get out in our time. Let's put our heads together and see what direction we could try."

"I don't know exactly." Patrick was hopeful that Eamon might give him some answers. "I walked east and made it to the ring fort."

"You didn't make it too far," said Conall. "Milliuc has friends there. They know his property and watch for him. Eamon here tried to head south a few years back and got caught by the same guards. North of here is another fort, smaller, but Milliuc has eyes there as well." He paused. "That was the way I tried."

Patrick listened to their tales with growing despondence. If Milliuc had lookouts posted around all of his borders, and to the west was a vast ocean, how could any of them hope to leave?

In the dark of night, his worst thoughts surfaced as he listened to the snores of his housemates. It's my punishment, he rationalized, for the sins of my past. He recalled the priest of Bannaven Taberniae warning the congregation of the wages of sin. A price would eventually have to be paid for his drinking and gambling with Linus. He was doomed to this living hell, giving thought to beliefs of God and sin he had rarely contemplated.

Each night, Patrick was struck by the monotony of his life. He worked all day at jobs which were never finished; he went to bed, slept uneasily, and woke up exhausted. No games with Linus, no interesting lessons from Dyfed. He didn't think they were interesting at the time but now he'd love to hear the history of the Empire, or be asked to recite Cicero. He earned small comfort from the warmth of the fire. Eamon and Conall grudgingly tolerated him, but they would never accept him. He was too foreign, too strange.

Occasionally, Dathi visited Milliuc. If Patrick was in sight, Dathi would give him a small nod but that was all. It was unspoken that the druid's storytelling visits to the pasture were to remain secret.

The winter months approached, gray and wet. Restricted to the farm, Patrick even began to miss limited freedom of the pasture. On the farm, threshing wheat, he'd never been so sore, nor worked so hard. His hands calloused and feet blistered. He couldn't stop thinking how drastically his life had changed since spring, and he longed for the simple comforts of home. His memories of silk pillows grew stronger, and he wished he had never taken them for granted. Maura crafted leather slippers for them all, but it was nothing compared to the strength of his Roman boots.

The tunic that Patrick had been wearing when he arrived was now thin and threadbare. It didn't do anything to stop the cold from seeping into his bones.

Maura worked late into the evening fashioning new breeches for him, softer leather than the shoes, and weaving a new woolen tunic. He was thankful for her consideration.

"Finally out of your nightshirt?" Eamon asked as they gathered for evening stew.

"Dathi insisted on it," said Maura. "He told Milliuc it was shameful to treat his servants in this way."

For some reason, the thought of Dathi as his protector irked him. He was tired of puzzling over the druid and his stories, wondering why he should care one way or another about the ancient Irish gods. His grandfather would be shocked. He should pray like a proper Christian and tell Dathi to go find some other slave to bother.

"Go away," he said, thinking of Dathi, not realizing he'd spoken aloud.

"What's that?" Maura handed him his bowl.

"Nothing," he tried to cover his mistake. "I was praying before our meal. To God." He quickly mentioned God—a cover that would have made sense at home in Britannia—but not here.

Eamon and Conall regarded him with narrowed eyes. Liam laughed.

"We have festivals for our gods," Liam informed him. "The druids talk to them for us."

"Well, Christians have only one God, and we say our own prayers," he replied, suddenly defensive of his childhood churchgoing, although he knew priests would gladly intervene with the prayer.

"Christians?" asked Conall. "What's that?"

None of them had heard of God or the Church or Jesus, he realized.

"The religion in Britannia, or at least the Roman part of it. One God, whose Son, Jesus, died for our sins."

"What's sins?'"

"Things you aren't supposed to do."

Conall rubbed his chin and looked warily at Patrick. "One god? But he's got his son along with him? Isn't that two gods, then?"

Patrick's head hurt. He didn't intend to get into any religious discussion with Conall. He was just trying to divert attention from his conversation with the invisible Brigid. "They're one in the same, God, his Son, the Holy Spirit."

"Their what?" Eamon had joined their conversation.

"Spirit. Soul. Ghost. The thing inside you."

"So it's three of them?" asked Eamon.

"No—we're not pagan like you. We don't have a hundred gods for each season. It's just God."

"And his son?" asked Conall.

"And the spirit?" asked Eamon.

"No!" Patrick stood up, frustrated. He couldn't explain the Trinity like his grandfather could. "They are all one."

Both men shook their heads at him and glanced at each other with a look that sealed Patrick's fate among them as a lunatic.

CHAPTER 19

Brigid

I awoke cold and naked in the center of the oak grove. The Test of the Ancients. Who would leave me in the forest like this? I might become prey for wolves and other wild animals. Then I saw the smoldering bonfire, still warm. I hadn't been alone for long.

Mother's words from the day before returned to me: *Maithghean can punish you in any way he sees fit.*

Punishment. Maithghean had his way.

I sat up on the wooden bench, which sent my head reeling. Bile rose in my throat. The aftertaste of the drug was still present. The Test left me feeling raw and cold after a night of confusing dreams and visions.

Shivering, I lay back down, curled into a ball. What happened? Every one of my muscles ached. Random images sizzled across my mind, like a shooting star in the night. I saw faces of people unknown, yet strikingly familiar. I now knew, with the slow recovery of memories, that they were faces of the Tuatha dé Danann.

The dream I had since childhood fell into place. I knew the Tuatha dé Danann. I had been one of them. *Help us*, they cried. I recalled my vision of them at Druin Criadh. They needed my help to return to the world. Somehow I was here, in this world, while the Danann retreated into hiding beneath the earth. It was me, yet not me. Pieces were missing, holes in the fabric of my history, lives layered on lives.

And the shepherd. The man with the staff. Who was he? What about him? Padraic? Patrick? There was something nagging, incomplete. All of this added up to past lives, another Brigid, but it still didn't make sense.

The Test did prove one thing. I was one who could remember a previous existence, a rare feat among druids. I didn't recall much, but it was a start. I pushed through the sickness and lingering fear and took a deep breath of self-satisfaction. With this gift, I would be a successful druid, possibly even head druid. The idea of replacing Maithghean one day pleased me. But it was Maithghean who interrogated me for information. I had to figure out what he wanted. He knew if this test succeeded, I could rival him for power, so why do it in the first place? Why not leave me ignorant of the past?

I sat up again in the misty morning fog, wondering if I should return home. Was the ritual over? Would anyone come for me? The fires were dying, their last wisps of smoke reached for the sky. Then I spied my cloak hanging on a low-lying branch of the old oak. My legs were weak and my stomach lurched as I reached for it.

Suddenly, it came to me. What had I told Maithghean? What questions had he asked? If he knew I had been—was—Danann, he would try to use my powers to his advantage, powers yet unrealized. This is what he tried to do my entire life. He wanted me to tell him the secrets of Danann magic, to tell him how the Danann could disappear as they did. I didn't know all of their mysteries, not yet. Their power is what he wanted.

I wrapped the wool around me, thinking about how to deal with the chief druid...thinking about how to tap into the Danann powers that were inherently mine. I couldn't challenge him until I remembered more.

I would need to protect myself, and I would need help. Blue eyes flashed before me. The shepherd. He promised to help me, long ago. This much I knew; this much I remembered.

No one mentioned the Test of the Ancients when I returned to the village. The druids acted as if it had never happened, even Father, though my mother seemed to seethe with a new anger.

Maithghean's eyes followed me, as though he searched for my secret. Fear swelled in the pit of my stomach, and the back of my neck needled under his gaze. He seemed particularly interested in my training and made excuses to enter Elían's lodge to ask about a bit of healing lore or to check on my progress. I felt him in my mind and in my solar plexus as he searched for my power. He would try to take it from me, as he did when I was a child. He couldn't put his hands on me as he used to, so he tried in different ways. I stood silent while Elían answered his questions and was relieved when he left.

"Why has he taken a sudden interest in my training?" I asked. We pounded herbs into a fine powder for medicines, and I enjoyed the thump thump of the mortar and pestle.

"He is the chief druid. It's his concern to know of your advancement."

I sifted through the lavender dust, pouring the contents into a stone container. I then put a handful of the dried leaves into a leather pouch I made for traveling.

"No, there is more to it," I protested. "He doesn't give Bacene the same attention."

"You are a healer. Your job is to save lives, a more important task than telling stories. Don't tell Tagdh or Bacene I said that." She winked like it was a joke between us. She sorted through the rafters full of dried plants: lavender, for its digestive properties, which also contained magical powers and was often used in druid ritual; alfalfa, with its purple stalks, was requested by many in the lean winter months to stave off hunger; caisearbhan was most powerful when it turned white in midsummer, its gentle seeds blown into the wind—now we dried for its potent brew. Father used the weed when its head was yellow and stem milky to assist in his prophecies.

"You haven't explained why Maithghean has to come in here every day to watch us work," I countered.

Elían's pounded more dried leaves into dust. Relations between us had been tense since the Test of the Ancients. Every night I searched my mind, trying to recall what I might have said in the drugged state, but it was a lost space of time. I panicked to remember what I said during the test.

"Your oddities," Elían continued her lecture, "have increased since the Test of the Ancients. Your father recounts the numerous nightmares you've had. You stop your work here and stare into the distance for minutes at a time. Maithghean is concerned."

I held back a sarcastic noise in my throat. Maithghean, I knew in the depths of my soul, wasn't concerned for my well-being.

"Elían, please, what happened during the test?"

"We're busy, Brigid. The plants must be ground by the full moon, and the newest ones you gathered have just set to dry."

"Elían, you must help me."

"You won't remember," she finally relented. "The drug is too strong."

"But you were there. You know what questions Maithghean asked me and what I answered." Desperate and frustrated, I couldn't understand why she refused to help.

Her back to me, she swept off the dusty shelves and emptied containers of old medicines to make space for the new ones. Medicines, I realized with appalling clarity, medicines that made the horrid paste.

A chill went down my spine. A voice whispered inside me: *Don't trust her.*

One day, I quietly approached an elderly couple at the market. The woman squinted and held plants and herbs close to her face.

"My sight's gone," Niamh told me. "And he's not much of a help." She waved her hand at her husband who stayed at her side. Niamh was bent and hunched from the years. Her husband and sons scratched a minimal existence, she said, from the forest. As her age advanced, her sight failed, and she could no longer see to make her tea. They were poor folk who visited the Fotharit market seasonally, then retreated back into the woods.

"I can get her what she needs," her husband said. "But I never remember which plant is which. She was the healer for those of us in the forest."

To get away from Maithghean and Elían's constant scrutiny, I took to leaving Fotharit for two or three days at a time. I traveled into Niamh's forest community and told Elían I was gathering plants. I wasn't sorry. I delivered herbs and food to the folk tucked away in the dark, forested country and who lived in a scattering of huts. They needed help most of all, and I shared with as many as I could. After a few visits, I showed those who were interested plants they could gather in their forest, taught them how to dry the plant, and store the herbs for use. Niamh introduced me to other healers in hidden enclaves. We met and shared herbal lore and plants from each other's regions.

I visited Niamh personally at each waxing moon, and brought her chamomile tea. I foraged for her and devised a system of drying leaves and roots so she could identify them. We decided to organize her drying rack by symptom, headaches, stomachaches, fever.

"Thank you again, Brigid."

"Now, this is mugwort," I placed the plant in her hand.

"Yes, I can feel the downy side of it." She brushed her finger over the thin hairs along the stem. I tied the plant carefully to its place on the drying rack.

"Next, here are bulbs of garlic. You know this by the smell and size. Add a clove or two every day to your meals. It will help keep illness away."

"*Saille*." She touched the rough willow bark. She used it often and knew its painkilling properties.

We spent afternoons organizing her pharmacopeia to her liking. I enjoyed the work. I didn't need Elían looking over my shoulder. I *knew* the plants and their properties. Even so, Niamh described to me new ways of concocting teas, and whether certain plants were better as whole leaves or grounded powder. I was happy to be away from Fotharit and found I was able to put the Test of the Ancients out of my mind, free from Maithghean's heavy stare.

On my next visit, I filled my cart with cheese and butter and gave the supplies to Niamh.

"You are too generous, Brigid." Her wrinkled hands grasped the cask of butter. Their only cow had died on the moon before, leaving them with no dairy. Father, Mother, and I had our own farm, three milk cows, a pasture of a dozen sheep and heifers, and a pen full of pigs. We also received the druid rations from the hunters, so there was always extra meat in our house.

"We have plenty, more than enough to share."

"Thank you again, Brigid. Stay with us tonight? It smells like rain soon."

"Oh, no thanks are needed." I was glad for the escape. I'd learned more from the forest folk than from Elían.

Niamh and I said our goodbyes, and I promised to return after the next full moon.

CHAPTER 20

Patrick

Samhain. Milliuc brought his family and servants to the ring fort. Inside, there was a formal ceremony by the druids, who circled around a large bonfire. The night was cold and clear.

Patrick stayed back against the stone wall that circled the village. He'd watch from a distance even though two warriors guarded him. He was glad to be away from work, but he had no intention of participating in the heathen ritual, dancing in a circle like a fool. He stared up at the stars in the sky instead. An eerie feeling crept over him as the druids chanted. The firelight cast shadows on their hooded faces.

He couldn't help but watch the ceremony, curious. Seven druid priests and priestesses in white robes lifted an animal toward the sky. A piglet squealed above the heat of the flames, its tiny legs kicked.

"Great Sow," a hooded priestess intoned. "We sacrifice this small gift to you, thankful for our harvest, our abundance of oats and corn to feed the people of Foclut Forest. Tonight, Mother Goddess, we ask for your protection through the winter's darkness. Watch over us, Mother of All."

She slit the piglet from throat to end in one swift movement. She pulled the entrails out of the dying animal and dropped bloody loops of guts and veins into an earthenware bowl. The druids believed entrails were powerful portents into the future. The sacrificer tossed the carcass on the flames and the acrid fumes of burning flesh filled the air. The druids bowed their heads in thanksgiving. Patrick's stomach heaved.

The tuath clasped their hands together, including the farmer and his servants. Patrick saw Eamon and Conall in the crowd, heads bowed willingly. Even Milliuc seemed to truly believe in the ceremony. Barbarians.

Hypocrite. Milliuc was a bigger hypocrite than the rest. Patrick knew what he did to Maura in the middle of the night. He'd step over the sleeping men, push aside her boys, and take her outside. Patrick heard the rough sounds and Milliuc's harsh whisper and groan. Maura would return to her bed, sometimes crying, other times silent. Bruises appeared on her face now and then.

Patrick watched as Maura stood next to Conall, her two children beside her. It's wrong, the whole thing is wrong, and I can't do anything about it.

He paced along the perimeter of the ring fort wall, and the two warriors followed close behind him.

"Tell me," he asked the men, since they wouldn't leave him alone. "What's this ceremony?"

"It's the end of the harvest year. The wheel of seasons is coming to a close, the death of the year," answered one warrior.

A chill swept through him. He paced again to stay warm. He refused to get any closer to the fire. He didn't want to be pulled into participation. The darkly cloaked druids, the blood on the knife blade... "The sacrifices with the animals. ..why?"

"The barrier between the living and dead is thin. The sacrifices protect us."

This made much sense as the priest at his church in Bannaven Taberniae. Jesus died on the cross for your sins, he recalled the old man saying. As a child, Patrick thought that was silly. Jesus doesn't know me. I didn't ask him to die for me. I shouldn't have to sit here every week because of it. He touched the cross in his pocket again and wished for the comfort of his grandfather's church, the clean white-washed walls, the gold chalice of wine for communion.

The druids circled the fire, hands clasped. Their eyes were closed and beads of sweat appeared on their brows. They invoked their goddess with all they possessed. They believed. Patrick didn't understand it, but they believed as much as his grandfather believed in communion.

He thought of his grandfather's prayers, recitations for different parts of the Mass. "Our Father, who art in Heaven, Hallowed be thy name..." The words comforted him. He hadn't thought of Mass in years, yet somehow these druids reminded him. He touched the cross in his pocket and continued the verse. "Thy Kingdom come, thy will be done..."

Thy will. Thy will! Whose "will" was it that he was trapped here on this godforsaken island? It didn't matter, he thought. He was still a slave. The next day would continue as the one previous, full of work and blistered hands. There was no way out.

The guards commanded that he wait for his housemates before returning to the farm. Milliuc and his family followed them from a distance, his wife and children laughing. It was the first time Patrick had seen Milliuc's wife, a fat woman with red cheeks, up close. She and her husband matched; they were a well-suited couple.

"Milliuc!" A voice called, stopping the retinue. Dathi, the druid.

"How can I help you?" The farmer was immediately contrite.

"I hear you had a grand harvest this year," Dathi said. His eyes were hidden in the depths of his hood.

"I did." Milliuc puffed up with pride. "I have fine land and strong workers." He motioned to his servants, who were silent in the presence of the druid. Eamon and Conall nodded respectfully and Patrick felt uneasy, how this man sought him out.

Dathi observed the men, and then pointed to Patrick. "This new one has brought you luck."

"Perhaps," Milliuc answered, but gave Patrick a narrow-eyed glare. Dathi's pointing him out would not make his life any easier with Milliuc.

Dathi came closer, making a circular gesture with his hand. Patrick grew nervous and tried to step back, but he froze in fear. He watched the gray eyes under the white hood, uncertain of the power behind them. Silent tension rose between Patrick and the man who spoke to the gods. He and the druid held eye contact while energy spun around them. He felt as if he were wrapped within a whirlpool, unable to escape.

Finally, Dathi smiled. "One day, Patrick will be a force to be reckoned with."

"Who? This shepherd lad?" Milliuc asked.

Patrick shrank back, uncomfortable with the attention paid to him.

Dathi waved his hand, as if brushing away a cobweb. The energy that had bound them together was gone. He turned to Milliuc, addressing him as if there had never been a pause in conversation.

"Well, whatever the cause for your abundant crops, you have yet to distribute the druids' share. Bring twelve sacks of grain to me tomorrow." He glared at Milliuc and stalked away while the farmer sputtered for words.

CHAPTER 21

Brigid

A messenger sent word to Mother about a new community, similar to those Conor spoke of, years ago. They built stone beehive huts on a northern beach and wanted new people to join them. A man named Erc was the leader and he was contacting slaves and servants in nearby villages. Mother and I were mixing oats for bannocks and just set the iron griddle over the fire to heat when the messenger arrived and recited his news.

"Thank you," she said when he finished. "Tell Erc my daughter and I would be glad to join them, if we can get permission to leave."

"Join them?" I asked, surprised. "Me?" I knew Mother wanted to go. I didn't realize I was supposed to go with her.

"I didn't want to say anything unless it actually happened. We have a chance for freedom, Brigid."

"But I'm in training." It sounded completely selfish. My mother was a servant, yes, but I was to one day be a druid.

She poured the oat mixture on the griddle and waited. "Brigid, do you understand druid-in-training or not, that you inherit my status?"

I understood, in the sense that she'd mentioned it before. Father alluded to it. But to be druid, besides it being my natural calling, would exempt me from the slave status. I would rise above that birth rank.

When I didn't answer, she continued, turning the bannocks over to cook on the other side. "You decide as you must. You're old enough to make your own decisions. But I don't trust Maithghean and what he might do to you. He already took you in the middle of the night for the Test, and there was nothing I could do. I spent my life here for you. I wanted to protect you." She clasped both of my hands in hers. "And I couldn't. They took you away and I couldn't stop them."

"I'm not hurt." In the many things I hadn't considered, I also hadn't thought about her guilt, how she must have felt when I was taken in the night. "There wasn't anything you could have done."

"I could have protected my daughter," she said, tracing her fingertip over my brow. "Listen to me. The effects of that test are still to come, Brigid. Listen to me well. The Test of the Ancients opens a portal to your past, whatever it may be. You will have memories, dreams, and visions that may confuse and weaken you."

"Weaken me? How?" I had spent the last days thinking I had succeeded because of the test, because I had survived the test.

"You're only at the beginning. Memories will arrive when you least expect it. I wouldn't be surprised if Maithghean tested you only to make you weak."

"How do you know this?"

"Once, when I was a child in Alba, a woman was tested similarly. She survived, but was sick for many months. Memories came upon her without warning. It must have been terrible. Her screams filled the village. Once, she grabbed me and spoke in a language I didn't know." Mother shuddered at the memory. "The druids were convinced of her past. She had been a healer who held the secret of a potent medicine. They were right, and she did remember."

"I saw things the night of the test," I said. "But like a dream, it makes no sense. Faces of people I don't know now, but I knew in the past, or will know in the future. I don't know who they are or why they are there."

"One day their meanings will become clear. It will be months or even years. People, events will come into your memory, maybe only one or two things at a time. Maithghean wants access to your powers, to whatever you hold from your past."

"What powers?" My brow burned when I was angry but I didn't know how to access them or even channel the powers - if they existed at all. I knew healing without much assistance from Elían.

"It will all take time. Months, years. Whatever comes to you, don't tell Maithghean. Do you promise me that?"

"I promise." Her words reinforced the fear already within me. I wondered if I should stay in Fotharit, without my mother.

"You can come with me but I can't promise you'll finish your apprenticeship. You will have to decide."

Maithghean had taken me, all the druids had taken me, in the middle of the night. The next decade or more of my life would be training with Father, Elían, and Maithghean. The same druids who drugged me in my sleep. The same ones who refused to explain the test they forced upon me.

"What if I leave?" I asked. I thought about what Mother had done. She sent messengers to find a community that would accept her. "Couldn't I learn with another druid order?" People didn't often change tuaths...but it seemed possible. I slid the bannocks off the griddle and into a basket that I would be taking to the forest community. Mother ladled out another round of mixture onto the griddle

"I don't know who would accept you. Training with another tribe once you've already begun here would be difficult. They're not your people, not your histories. And not many druids will go against Maithghean."

I changed the subject. "Are you sure you want to leave and live with the Palladians? They're Christians, of the Roman belief."

"I will be free, Brigid. Do you know what that means to me?"

"But you don't believe as they do. Conor said it was only for the people called Christians."

"I have nothing against what they say, and I'd like to learn more. There's more to it, Brigid. I'm going because I have kin there. You have kin there."

"Who?"

"Some of the people who had been taken from Alba with me, including my brother. I will return to them. It's better than arguing with your father day in and day out. I look forward to not seeing Sena's sneer every time I go to the village. I'll have my freedom. I'll be with my family." Family. Her people. My people. I hadn't fully understood all my mother had lost.

"What about Father?" I asked.

"I loved your father. I still do. I believed that love could survive anything." She looked me squarely in the eye. "It can't, Brigid. Remember what I tell you. Love can't survive pettiness and jealousy. It can't survive being ignored. Eventually, the flame will die if it is not cared for properly." She and my father had fought since my childhood, arguments never resolved. Father refused to change his marital situation, and she refused to accept it. Now, I had to decide what to do. Stay here in my home, or join my mother in her new life.

She continued, "I was jealous of Sena. I tried to trust your father's words. He ignored my requests and my feelings. He doesn't know what it's like to have that woman belittle you, while he didn't do anything about it.

"That is the most hurtful part, Brigid. Not once did your father stand up for me in public. Remember, years ago, when you and Bacene fought at the Imbolc festival? Here in the house, over discussions with Maithghean, he would vouch for me. Never outside these doors did he acknowledge me as his partner." She bowed her head, but didn't cry.

"I don't want you to go." I said. It was childish. Selfish.

"You can come with me."

"But my studies..." Back to what held me here. I was years into my druid training. To give it up now seemed impossible.

"It is my one regret, Brigid. I never finished my training in Alba because of the raid that put me here. Finish it if you can, but I worry about your safety."

"I can handle Maithghean," I said. "I've managed so far, except for the Test itself." But even then, he didn't learn everything. He didn't gain the powers from me that he wanted. Otherwise, he wouldn't be following my every lesson with Elían, questioning me about every visit to the forest.

Decision made, Mother and I finished making the bannocks, and sat quietly together to watch the glow of embers in the hearth.

CHAPTER 22

Patrick

Sheep shearing was a job that needed to be done before Patrick took the sheep to pasture. But Milliuc insisted the pregnant ewes be sheared now, even though it was still winter, cold and damp. The lambs would be born in a few weeks, Milliuc explained. It was best to get the pregnant ewe's wool before they birthed, making a somewhat cleaner birth process. The rest of the flock would wait until the warmer days of spring.

Patrick had no idea what to do. He'd never sheared before. He shivered at the idea of taking a blade to the gentle animals, even though it was just their wool. Milliuc crammed himself into the small shed with the servants to push the animals forward in the shearing line.

Milliuc pushed Maura aside as he struggled to organize the animals. His action filled Patrick with hatred. Maura wasn't only his friend but a fellow Briton. He felt for her as he did Brawen. Milliuc's treatment of her was wrong. Forced labor was wrong. Brigid was right. There had to be another way to do things, without slaves.

Then, he thought of his servants in Britannia, of the boy Darys whom he had ordered around from morning until night. He never questioned Darys's purpose. He had never asked where Darys was from. Not once did he consider that Darys might have a family he missed. Patrick directed part of his anger toward himself, a belated guilt.

Patrick ran a blade over the whetstone and sharpened metal caught his eye. He tested the edge of the blade with his thumb. He drew blood. The shearing blade could cut the farmer's throat easily. Patrick glanced at Milliuc, who studied the animals in their pen, deciding which to shear first. He could slit Milliuc's throat in one swift gesture, almost painless. Then they would all be free: Maura and her children...Eamon could return to his home...Conall too...He would save more lives than he took. Patrick's pulse quickened as he walked toward Milliuc with the knife. It would be so quick, and then...

Drop it. A voice not his own. A woman's voice. He released the knife. It clattered to the ground.

Milliuc turned at the noise. "You've no skill at all, do you, boy? Pick up your tools. We'll start with this ewe; you've got to be gentle with them now. It will give you good practice for shaving the rams in the spring."

He waded into the pen, motioning for Patrick to follow. Patrick held the retrieved blade in his grip, fingers tightening as he stood knee-deep in wooly animals.

Killing with the blade would be messy. Difficult with the sheep underfoot. Killing. The word hit hard.

Milliuc pulled a pregnant ewe aside and pulled prickly thistles from her coat. "Here you go, lad. Start like this, getting off what you can. We can't be selling it or weaving it full of pasture grass."

Patrick followed his master's motions, cleaning the wool, but continued to grip the shearing blade in his other hand. He knelt down next to the animals, burying his face in the thick wool.

You don't want to do this, Patrick.

He loosened his hold on the blade, allowing it to slip to the floor. His hands shook as he picked thorns out of the wool.

"Now," Milliuc said, out of breath from his struggle with the sheep. "I'll show you how to shear one of these dumb beasts. You and Liam will do the rest of the pregnant ones today. Maura will pick up the wool for carding."

Patrick nodded and forced his eyes to look at the several dozen ewes as he bit down on his rage.

In one swift move, Milliuc had the sheep at a right angle, forcing her to the ground. He held her head and knelt partially on her back as he quickly shaved her front brisket and over the left shoulder. Keeping her on her side, he sheared the top of her head, shoulder and neck as the poor animal squirmed.

Milliuc pulled her up, almost comically, into a sitting position and sheared down her left side. He then lifted her front legs, running the blade over her swollen belly before he turned the animal again, pressing her head with his chest, so he could reach her back flank. Milliuc reached along her backbone and downward as he finished one-half of the job. He stood, legs bracing against the ewe, and nodded to Patrick.

"She's half done; now you do the rest." He handed his blade back to Patrick. Patrick watched the expert shearing and doubted he'd be successful at slitting the man's throat. Milliuc was quick with the knife.

He took the knife and Milliuc's place at the ewe's belly and straddled her, pressing hard. He used too much force, and the animal noticed the change in master. She struggled to her feet.

"No, no, no!" Milliuc yelled. "Grab her before she gets away!" Patrick lunged to grab her, but tripped and fell, flat on his face. The half-naked ewe escaped into the yard, dancing wildly at her success. Liam, on his way to join them, saw the commotion and made a dash for the ewe. He grabbed her by the wooly side and dragged her back into the barn.

Patrick picked himself up off the floor, and Milliuc shook his head in disappointment.

"Dathi said you were a force to be reckoned with, but by the gods above and below, boy, I don't see how."

Even Liam giggled. "You're a rich Roman boy, never done a day's work in your life. You couldn't even feed the animals last year, and you can't catch them this year."

Patrick dusted off his breeches, his face aflame. He took the animal from Liam and held her under her chin as Milliuc doled out instructions.

Liam, who had assisted with the previous year's shearing, sped along, lost in the piles of dirty white wool. After the fourth or fifth sheep, Patrick began to feel comfortable with the task. The shearing was hard, hot work. He threw himself into it, letting his anger out. He hated Milliuc. He would have killed him, or tried to, if he hadn't been interrupted by the voice. Interrupted by... he would have to ask Dathi. He flipped the ewe to her other side. It was foolish to trust a voice, a spirit, a ghost. Or, more than likely, his imagination, or a sickness, a result of getting his head bashed so many times.

He pulled the sheep to her upright position so he could work on her belly. He finished shearing and pushed the animal toward the door. He laughed as the pink-skinned ewe ran outside and munched happily on the green grass.

"You've finally caught on," said Liam. "Like you've done this in your past life."

Past Life. Dathi had mentioned that belief. The smell of lanolin and wool seemed familiar, but he refused to acknowledge Liam's comment. The idea of a past life was just too foreign. If he admitted belief, then he'd admit a commonality with the druids, and with Dathi. That man made his skin crawl.

Patrick began to shear the next animal. He slipped his thumb into the sheep's mouth as Milliuc instructed and held the ewe's head back. Again and again, he sheared, until there were no more animals in line. He looked around the empty barn, arms sore, covered in nicks and cuts.

"Are you done? Put your tools away then." Liam stowed his blade on the tool shelf and motioned for Patrick to do the same. Patrick snapped out of his daze and looked again at the shearing blade. He would have killed Milliuc, in defense of Maura, if something unnamed hadn't stopped him. He'd hated another man, long ago, just as much. He didn't know who; he couldn't identify a name. Only a feeling that this had happened before, like with the language. He carried the blade to the cupboard and placed it carefully on the shelf, wondering if one day he would have the nerve to use it.

The following day, Patrick began his next project, bundling the loose wool and tying it with rope. Liam barely had to show him how to bind the rope. He had done this before. He didn't remember it as a memory, but as a feeling. It wasn't details of an experience he recalled; he only had the knowledge.

A dusting of snow melted from the ground in thin patches. The cold air was welcome as he rolled a load of wool together and wiped his brow. He tried doing as Dathi said. If he could pray to God, he could speak to these Danann folk.

"What if the Danann can't return?" he asked. Maybe the fairies heard.

"Who are you talking to?" Liam demanded as he approached with a wagon cart. Patrick flushed. He'd spoken aloud. Again.

They lifted bales of wool into the cart. "God," he replied. He decided the Christian reference was a better answer than admitting he talked to an ancient Irish god.

"Holy boy, you are always praying," Liam said. "As if you were a druid yourself."

Patrick bristled at the jibe. He was no druid. The thought of the Samhain sacrifice, and of Dathi's sea-gray eyes, made him shiver.

"Why do you pray?" The boy tied cords around a heap of cream-colored wool.

"There's nothing else to do. The sheep don't talk to me." Patrick tried to make a joke, but Liam was serious.

"I talk to you," the boy said.

Patrick scratched the scruff of his new beard. The wool stuck to his whiskers.

"Yes, you do, Liam. And for that I'm very thankful. But when I'm alone up there on the hillside –" he pointed to the rocky outcropping above the farm. "I've got no one else to talk to but God." He pulled the makeshift cross from his pocket and showed Liam.

"This is a symbol of my God. His son died on a cross like this."

Liam held the twigs and turned them over in his hand. "Why did he die on a cross?"

"Well, back then, the Romans didn't like him and convicted him of treason. They believed he wanted to betray the Roman government and start a revolt. They tied criminals to posts like this to die, as their punishment."

Liam handed it back. "Do you talk to those sticks too?"

"Sometimes I do. They give me strength. If Jesus could handle his suffering on the cross, then I can handle this." Patrick lifted the next bale of wool into the wagon. He hadn't really believed it until he said it. Then the idea of talking to the fairy people seemed utterly ridiculous. What had he been thinking?

"You can talk to the na daoine sí if you're that bored up there, instead of talking to sticks," Liam said. "The fairy woman lives in those hills."

Patrick took a deep breath. This is what Dathi talked about. The ancient gods changed to fairy belief. It couldn't hurt to find out more. It would give him something to consider when was sent out to pasture again, all alone. "All right, Liam, what sorts of stories do you know about the fairy people?" He refused to mention the druids. Thoughts of the hooded priests and their animal sacrifices unnerved him. Dathi and his conversations were one thing, but all of them, together, circling the fire sent chills through him. But he wanted to know more. Dathi was always talking about the Danann, about Brigid, how he, Patrick, must remember this woman.

"Just if I'm bad, the fairies will take me underground with their magic." Liam backed away from him and took refuge behind a large bale of wool. "That's what Conall tells me."

"Tell me what you know about those who live underground," Patrick asked. "Do they ever come out? Do they talk to people?"

"I don't know. I've never talked to one. I'd be too scared to. Ask mam, ask Conall. All I know is that the fairies live underground, hidden there after people came to Éire."

"What do they call the fairies? What is their tribe?"

"The Tuatha dé Danann. They're the fairy folk."

"What else do you know about the Danann, Liam?"

The boy went back to his work, keeping his distance from Patrick, and tied twine around another bale of wool. "Some of them are the old gods and some of them are fairies. You'll have to ask someone else. I don't really know."

Patrick corralled the sheep into their pens and considered his upcoming return to the pasture. During the winter, he was part of the busy life on the farm. People were constantly around him; he was surrounded at meals, at bedtime. Chatter and snores became a background drone, like the buzz of honeybees. He craved solitude, yet dreaded loneliness. No sooner did he think this did Dathi appear in the shearing shed where Patrick tied and stacked the ewe's wool.

"You've recalled your childhood in Britannia." Dathi cut through his angry thoughts. "Can you go back farther? Can you remember more?"

Frustrated, Patrick kicked a clod of frozen mud out of his way. "I'm a slave for the rest of my life. This is it, no more, no less. Nothing matters—escape plans, this ceremony—none of it matters."

"Look at what you've endured. And Maura—you have a compassionate character." Dathi reached for a bale of wool and situated himself on it, readying for a long conversation.

"Maura? I don't—I mean, I haven't..." he stopped, confused.

"You don't pity Maura, and that is important. You genuinely want to help her."

"Well, of course! Wouldn't anyone?"

"If they feel anything, it's pity. Most accept the way things are. You're different. You want change. You even believe change is possible."

"I suppose I do." Change would mean freedom, returning to Britannia.

"Every time you speak to Maura or Conall or Eamon about escape, you give them hope. You help them to see that our island doesn't have to be this way. It hasn't always been this way. When the Danann ruled the island, no one was enslaved."

"You want everyone to go back to some ancient time in the past?" Patrick stacked another bale. He wondered if Milliuc knew of Dathi's presence on his farm. Probably not.

"I want you to go back to that time, to search your memories. You can show people how it used to be and how it can be again. You will change Éire."

Patrick shook his head. "You keep saying that," he said plaintively. "I don't see how."

As much as the druid annoyed him, speaking to Dathi gave him a conversation that revolved around more than sheep. Still, he reminded Dathi of his goal to return home, not teach Irishmen about their ancient gods. "I'd like a proper bath. I'd like a proper tunic. I'd even welcome church, if it would make my grandfather happy. I'd like to be part of a proper government."

Dathi laughed bitterly. "Rome fell long ago, before you were born," he said. "There's barely a shred of government left."

"There's enough. My father collected taxes for it. We had a nice home." He hoped his home had survived, that there was a place for his parents to return to after the raid.

"There is a reason you are here," Dathi always reminded him at the end of their conversations. The hooded man slipped out of the shed, unnoticed by anyone else.

The hills, encapsulated with ice, were a dull brown under the sheen. If there was a reason for all of this, Patrick couldn't figure out what it was. He had nothing to offer. He was a slave, trapped. If he ever escaped, if he were ever freed, he would leave and go home. There was nothing that would make him return to this island of damp and fog. He sat shivering in the animals' corral on the farm, as the fat sheep bleated their discontent at the weather.

"Brigid?" The origins of her name finally came to him when Dathi visited next and began another story. He'd slipped into the lambing shed. Patrick wondered at the druid's slyness, his ability to appear and leave so quickly. He had racked his memory and recalled what Liam had said about Brigid. "They have a ceremony. When the lambing begins, we have to prepare the animals for the festival."

Part of his puzzle was his being constantly harassed by this druid even though he was raised Christian. At least if God spoke to him, it would make more sense. And He'd probably have the manners to use good Latin. None of this Irish tongue. No goddess of the earth or of wheat fields or of ewe's milk.

"They have ceremonies, but they don't mean anything. Not anymore. War and divisions tear our land apart!" Dathi shook his fist, nearly reaching the thatched roof of the animal shed. "This is why we need you. How often has this village been raided for cattle? How many men have died?"

Quite often, Patrick thought. His fellow servants were here because of lost cattle raids. Not that he cared about the fate of the cows one way or another.

"Why me? If these brutes want to kill each other over cows, what am I to do about it?"

"Milliuc is an example of the problems Éire faces since the loss of the Danann. Tribalism. Rivalries. Instead of coming together, clans raid each other for cattle. People no longer connect with the earth. They've forgotten the power of the Danann. The idea of making a human form elemental with nature brings a shiver of fear, if not laughter, to most. But it's in the blood of our people! And they have forgotten."

"They are not my people. You keep saying that, but I have no ties to anyone here, unless it was someone else from my family that was also made a slave."

"You won't be a slave forever. You've saved the Danann before. You only need to remember all that you are and who you have been."

He leaned against the stone walls of the sheep pen. The animals bleated and milled around him. "I am Patrick of Bannaven Taberniae. My father is a prefect. My grandfather, a deacon. We are a well-respected family. I was training for the soldier's honor guard when Irish savages interrupted my life. Now I am a slave. There is nothing I can do, no one I can save."

"Think about your journey on the sea. You told me you were able to save Brawen from a terrible fate."

"But not Lupida and Darceca." Or myself, he added silently.

"There is only so much you can do at one time."

He pounded his fist into the dirty straw. "Right. Only so much. The only thing I'm meant to do now is feed these animals some grain. That's all. That's my purpose."

"Your purpose now, today, is to remember your past, not just the one in Bannaven Taberniae. You have many pasts."

It was the same argument that he insisted on him remembering something or someone from another time. It was pointless to argue.

CHAPTER 23

Brigid

Relief spread across the tuath on the day my mother left Fotharit. Her presence had been a source of stress for years, even if it wasn't her fault.

"There is nothing here for me," she said to Father. "We have no marriage. Brigid is grown."

She had to have Father's permission, and Dunlang's. As chief, Dunlang didn't have to allow her leave, but Mother and Father's situation had been an embarrassment for years. After consulting with Father and Maithghean, they all agreed. Dunlang announced her impending departure and Sena smirked at me in the village each morning as I traded our eggs. She had the decency, though, to keep quiet.

The messenger returned for Mother at the next full moon. With a few satchels of her belongings tied to a mule's saddlebags, Mother left with him.

I divided my time between visiting Niamh and my formal lessons with Elían. When I returned from the forest communities, Maithghean summoned me. He did this every time I returned from bringing medicines to Niamh.

"What did you bring her this time?"

"Mugwort. Willowbark. Same as before."

"Are you taking our supplies?"

My brow burned at the insinuation that I was stealing from the druids. "I've done extra foraging on my own to help Niamh."

"Why can't the old woman can't find her own herbs in the forest?" Maithghean's interrogation continued. He knew perfectly well why Niamh needed help. I didn't answer and waited for his next question.

"Elían tells me she never taught you about these plants."

Again, I said nothing.The truth was, I no longer needed her teaching. I knew the properties and how the herbs performed when seeped or boiled, when made into a tea or pounded into a powder. I was prepared for his questions. Maithghean would try any way he could to find out what I recalled from the Test.

What he didn't know is that I didn't know. Knowledge just came to me now, after the Test, as if I had always known. All I could recall with rote memory was images and emotions. Some I recognized, but most I didn't. It would take hours of meditation to make sense of the confusion and, as Mother warned, there were more memories to come. Keeping quiet gave me a slight edge over him. Let him believe there was something to discover.

I glanced around his home, stark and barren compared to ours. His home missed the presence of women. No loom filled with wool or pots of dye to add colors in the room. Wooden shelves leaned against the thatch, filled with stones, feathers, and mysterious sealed pots. He had only a bench and table and a small pallet in the corner. Herbs dried from the rafters. Implements of sacrifice were stacked in a dark corner, I saw, as a flash of light gleamed on metal.

I turned to leave and cast a distrustful eye at the clay pots filled with poisons and potions.

"I was sad to see Brocca go," the chief druid called after me. I spun on my heel, immediately incensed.

"She left because of you!"

"What do I know of her problems with your father?"

"You are the cause of their problems! You refused to grant her rank; you refused to perform a Beltane marriage for them."

Maithghean smiled and crossed his arms over his chest. I stood in the open doorway, knowing I should leave, but couldn't. I was too angry and he knew it. The sunlight filtered in, glinting off the gold torc he wore. It matched the glow emanating from the crown of my head. Maithghean squinted at me in the sunlight. Instinctively, I tied my hood around me.

"Brigid, there is much you don't know. Sena refused to accept your mother. That you do know. But your father never requested a formal divorce from Sena. Without either of those things, how am I supposed to perform the marriage ceremony?"

"I was there when Father said you had refused, many times, to marry them," I protested.

"You know the law. He and Sena never divorced. She refused and he didn't demand it. And—for some reason—Dubhtach wouldn't take your mother as a second wife, out of respect for Sena's wishes. The situation is so confusing the Brehons can't figure it out. They have been living together for so long...besides Dubhtach was only required to provide for you. What sort of ceremony should I have performed? Nothing fits their situation." Maithghean stared at me with a bemused look. I won't accomplish anything here, I warned myself. I should leave.

He sat, smug, waiting for this information to sink in. The pieces came together, the words of my parents' arguments. That is why Mother is leaving, because Father wasn't able to stand up to Sena. He wasn't able to stand up to Maithghean.

"I'm sure," I said coldly, "that you had your own reasons for keeping things as they were. You wanted my mother for yourself."

Maithghean glared at me now, and I returned his gaze. We were at war. Our animosity, long hidden, was now out in the open.

"I didn't want Brocca. She is a meaningless bondservant, not worth my time," he scoffed. "She was pregnant, however, with a child prophesied for greatness." He met me in the doorway. His yellow eyes filtered in the reflection of the sun. His single finger traced the edge of my hood. "All the druids knew you were to be born with gifts beyond our reach. I didn't want to marry Brocca; what I wanted, Brigid, was you."

We froze together at that moment. *What I wanted was you...* A pull in my mind and a sinking in my gut told me memories were about to take hold. I broke free and ran from his doorway as swiftly as I could. I was sick, consumed by revulsion for this old man I hated so much. Maithghean didn't want my mother for marriage or for lust. He wanted me. He wanted my abilities, my past, things I couldn't even access for myself.

I ran to the open fields beyond the tuath. Mother warned me this would happen, that the memories could appear at any time.

Another face flashed before my eyes; the man who showed himself in the Test of the Ancients. Bres. The name unlocked itself from my memory. Rapidly, images of him coursed through my brain. He had once tried to kill me on the battlefield, long ago, but then he was my husband. I saw us, with a child. I saw us again, sword to sword.

I found a spot to hide among the lambs. I poured my energies into the earth, asking for guidance. I tried to steady my breath and willed my mind to clear. I had to make sense of the Test. I saw faces of Ancient people, the Tuatha dé Danann. Maithghean had triggered something to bring the thoughts forward.

More images of Bres appeared, making me dizzy. I remembered Bres when he was young, his amber eyes and black hair. He was my husband, my lover, and he could be unspeakably cruel. He tried to take over the Danann. He would have killed them all if they hadn't joined together to stop him. A boy died because of him. My boy, my son. A gaping hole opened up within me. A wail. My lament. The futility of going on without him, locked in this past memory, lifetimes ago that felt like the present.

CHAPTER 24

Patrick

N ial went with Patrick when he brought the sheep back to pasture again. The freckle-faced boy ran alongside him, herding the ewes, excited to have the responsibility of a new chore. He'd grown tall and gangly over the years, Patrick realized. How many years? He'd lost count.

Patrick was glad to be out of the cramped quarters where Eamon and Conall watched his every move and complained about his sleep-talking about God or gods. He reached the summit of the hill and saw his lonely hut, untouched since harvest. Its dull straw was offset by the brilliant red fuchsia that grew along the base of the hut. The green fields were dotted with purple heads of clover. Solitude would eat at him unless Dathi appeared, a visit Patrick didn't know he'd welcome or not. While the druid's visits had definitely relieved his boredom, he didn't know if it was worth all the stories about the Irish gods and goddesses.

Dear Lord, he prayed. *Please help me make it through another season. Better yet, help me to escape.*

Nial guided the animals into their summer pen.

"Thank you, Nial."

The boy waited expectantly for a reward for his extra work. Patrick handed him a bit of bread and the boy ran off.

Now, alone in his summer pasture, he contemplated escape again. Two of his back teeth were missing and there was an unpredictable ringing in his ears.

He planned escape routes for lack of anything else to do. He strategized by drawing maps in the mud. He laid out elaborate patterns with sticks and blades of grass. Sometimes his maps directed him east, sometimes west. Both pointed him toward water, harbors, and ships.

His next attempts were futile, and the results were the same. Two warriors bound and beat him, and he awoke aching and sore in his hut. Liam and Nial arrived the following morning to make sure he was able to work, and that was that. Milliuc never admonished him personally, but left the discipline to his guards.

"Milliuc should sell him," one warrior said as they dumped Patrick's bruised body on his pallet for the third time that summer. Not counting the summer before, and the one before that, nor the previous one.

"He can't now. Dathi has forbidden it. That old druid has this one marked for something."

Patrick sat on the edge of his pallet, head in his hands. Dathi again. He was the reason Milliuc kept him, despite his numerous attempts to run away, year after year.

Eventually, Dathi found him as he had before, nursing his wounds in the shepherd's hut, holding a water-soaked rag to his forehead.

Dathi brought another basket of bread and cheese. He also handed Patrick a waterbag and several pouches filled with some kind of bark. "Willowbark," said Dathi. "Drink it as a tea for your headaches."

Patrick took a sip from the waterbag, which was already filled with the tea. "Are you here to give me more lessons?"

"Lessons, stories, whatever you'd like to call it. Really, I want you to remember..." He lay his hand over Patrick's brow, where there was a particularly bad cut. "Them beating you like this doesn't help."

Patrick wanted to roll his eyes at the druid but even the thought of the movement made his head ache even more. Dathi kept his hand on Patrick's forehead. The spot he touched seemed to warm, a healing warmth that spread and lessened the pounding against his skull.

"So. Everything the druids do is about time and the seasons," said Dathi." People need the gods' help at harvest or at planting."

"Enough talk of gods." Patrick went outside to sit in front of his hut. He should follow the sheep and begin to camp, but he'd round them up for one more night. Dathi followed. Of course. "What can I do exactly? You keep telling me these stories about these people, about their magic and battles and how Bres nearly destroyed them all. What does this have to do with me? What can I do?"

"You could bring it all back. Their power and yours. I can't reach it for you; it's yours. You have to remember for yourself

"I haven't remembered anything. I'm listening to your stories…but that's all."

"You listen, but you fight against me. You resist what I'm telling you, what used to be true."

"It is a little far-fetched. People blending into trees? Into rocks? Living underground with no concept of time? Seriously, Dathi."

"Can you stop fighting what I say?"

"Fine." Patrick walked down the hillside and rested his head on the lush grass. He had to admit, listening to Dathi was easier than reviewing Caesar's campaigns with Dyfed. "There came a time when new people appeared on our island. They found our sacred land, without our knowledge. It was a foreboding sign of what was to come."

"Our forebears hid the secret weapons of the Danann," Dathi explained. "Only the elders knew how to access the magic."

Patrick pondered the history, comparing the Danann battle tactics with Roman. Why didn't Nuada, this great leader, use the weapons at his disposal? Why keep them hidden, magical or not? The great Julius Caesar would have never let the enemy advance so far.

"Nuada refused to use the hidden weapons. He wouldn't use the stone of destiny, the Lia Fail, to her fullest advantage. Was that a smart move, militarily?" Dathi asked.

"The stone of destiny? He should have used every available tool to his advantage, even if it is a 'magical' rock." Patrick relied on his background of Roman military training. If the stories Dathi told him were true, the naiveté of the Danann was their downfall. No wonder they went into hiding.

"Yes, the stone spoke to the kings," continued the druid. "And when fighting drew near, she protested the killing with her entire voice. Years later, the Danann fought the Fomorians again because of Bres. We were all tricked by Bres," he said. "But, in the end, Bres got what he deserved, but it was too late for the Danann losses."

A lamb bleated, interrupting their warfare analysis. Patrick ran down the hill to find its back leg was wedged in a gap between two sharp stones. The mother ewe was by his side, baa-ing, unable to help. Patrick pulled the lamb from the crevice. Finally freed, the lamb and ewe stumbled together down the hillside, joining the rest of the flock.

"How do you think the Danann could have prevented the kingship of Bres?" Dathi asked when he was done with his task.

"I'm tired of the history lessons," Patrick groaned as he lay back on the thick warm grass. "My mind aches, I'm bruised all over, and all you've done is talk philosophy and war craft."

"Bres did eventually get to rule as he schemed and plotted, but it was only possible because of his marriage to Brigid."

Patrick sat up. He *knew* this. That was it, a brief inkling, but he grasped at it. A feeling like...jealousy? It made no sense. "I need to tend to the sheep, Dathi. I don't need to give Milliuc another reason to send those warriors down to me."

"You remembered, didn't you?" Dathi's smile took up his entire face.

"I didn't remember anything."

"Stop thinking of the memory in your mind. You feel the past with your spirit, your intuition." This time Dathi touched the center of his chest. His touch burned and Patricked jumped back.

"Leave me, druid."

Dathi's smile stayed on his face, even as he pulled up the hood of his robe. "Fine. The summer pasture is yours. But don't forget what I've told you. Pay attention."

Dathi left, and silence sat with him until sundown. He made camp for the night. Alone, he lit a torch with the embers he kept from the previous night's fire. He moved quickly as he gathered firewood along the dark border of the forest. Brigid...that name...the feeling in the center of his being. He stayed along the forest's edge as he listened to the howls of wolves.

CHAPTER 25

Brigid

The druids watched me as I shared food with poor families, to my friend Lomman and his mother, Una. The druids watched, disturbed, as I filled the wagon with cheese to bring to the forests. Elían, this time in front of all the druids, questioned my knowledge of medicines.

"I've never taught you this blend of powders," she said. "How did you know it would work for Dunlang's fever?"

"I don't know," I answered. I just *knew*.

The druids prepared for Samhain. We practiced the ritual in the sacred oak and discussed changes. Tagdh wanted new chants, Elían wanted silent contemplation. We circled the bonfire in our traditional spiral but the rhythm of the chants were off.

"Meditation then," said Maithghean , though meditation had never been his preference. He preferred the theatrics of fire and sacrifice.

We sat in our circle around the bonfire as he invoked the souls of those who had departed this year. We closed our eyes, picturing those our tribe had lost. Then he continued. "We call to the Ancient Ones. Join us at Samhain. Be part of our tribe. The veil is thin, the gate is open..." My brow burned at his words.

Everyone sank deeper into the mediation. We matched our breathing, and formed a link from one druid to the next. I allowed the fire to fill my brow and the heat coursed through me. I tapped into something deeper. I'd found it, the start of it, the ancient source. I sank into the earth, grounding in meditation. I could go deeper if I chose. I could disappear if I chose. I could go beyond where

Maithghean led. I could take the shape of stone and felt myself forming...part of me sank, blended, became one with the stone.

And then I felt it. A thought that wasn't my own. Something else, someone else sought inside of me, wanted to know how I became the stone. Searching. I pushed against it and it pushed back. Maithghean. I had a newfound ability and he wanted it. I gathered strength from the earth and forced him back. I opened my eyes, gasping and breathless in the circle. The others still had their eyes closed in meditation, all except for Maithghean. He nodded to me from across the fire. He'd found the door to my past and he would push it as hard as he could.

After the Samhain ceremony, the druids came for me again. Mother was right. They would not stop. They bound my hands with rope in the middle of the night. I struggled and understood that Father had let them in. They tried to force the bittersweet drugs into my mouth. Another Test of the Ancients. Test after test? This was unheard of. I bit down until I tasted blood. A voice cried out. Elían's. Fire burned in my skull as they tried to tie my hands again until a corner of that thatch wall behind my bed singed with smoke and sparked with flame.

"Leave me." A voice rose out of me but It was something greater than me that spoke, beyond me. The fire provided enough light for me to see Father, Maithghean and Elían. "Leave me."

Then, the smell of smoke. What had started as a spark spread.

"Fire!" someone cried. We all were startled. Lomman burst open the door and stopped short, seeing me with my hands bound with the three druids. "I was bringing in the cattle and saw the flames!" Fire spread up the wall toward the roof while those of us inside stood frozen with our secret.

"Come with me, Brigid," Lomman said. "You can stay with us." He took me by the bound hands, leading me away from the speechless druids. Villagers rushed past us with buckets to fill with water from our well, determined to extinguish the fire. Where the druids had gone, I didn't know.

I followed Lomman and the cattle to the tuath. He was Dunlang's herder now and brought the cows in from the fields every day to a pen where the chieftain kept his best animals. My eyes still burned from the smoke and my mouth tasted awful, a combination of herbs and blood. I wanted to be a druid, and blessed and initiated druid and I couldn't do it without them. I had defended myself so far, I had reasoned. And Maithghean wouldn't kill me. He couldn't because he wanted what I had. I ignored my memories of the past, I ignored each interrogation, I ignored each time he tried to pry inside my mind.

The next morning, Father found me as I walked with Una to the market. People asked how I was and I was glad for their concern. Even Moina waved to me from the front door of her mother's house, Elían nowhere to be seen.

"Our house is going to need significant repairs," Father said. "The back wall and part of the roof is burned through but the builders think they can save it. I'll stay with Maithghean until the house is fixed."

"Fine. I'll stay here in the village." My wrists were raw from rope burns.

"Let's talk about what happened, Brigid," said Father. Una left me to sell her eggs. I'm sure she wanted to be far from any druid.

"I'm not going to Maithghean 's house," I said.

"You don't have to. We need to sort out many things, Brigid, you and I. I should have done it after your mother left."

We went to the boulder we visited so often when I was a child. The wind was brisk and we kept our plaids wrapped tightly around us. We climbed the boulder and I wondered what he would say.

"How did the fire start, Brigid?"

"I don't know. You had my hands tied and were trying to poison me."

"No one was trying to poison you. It was an acolyte ceremony."

"Oh, a surprise ceremony just for acolytes? Where was Bacene?"

"Already at the oak grove with Tagdh." His lie stunned me. There was no ceremony like this. I closed my eyes and went deeper, to a previous past, and I knew this was all a lie. "You haven't answered my question about the fire."

I did know my brow had burned with anger. But house fires weren't uncommon. A stray ember from a cooking fire, thatched straw put up wet that combusted. "I don't have an answer to your question. I don't have an answer as to why my father would feed me poison."

For a long time, Father was silent, and said nothing. He stared at his hands. Hands that should have been throwing sticks or carving symbols, hands that had the power to divine the future. Finally, he spoke. "You know, Brigid, you are born with your mother's status. She was a slave. Dunlang gave her leave to join her Christian cult, but she is, according to the Brehons, still a slave, still my servant." The air stilled. Not a single branch stirred on the bare-branched tree above us. "I raised you as my own, even when Maithghean tried to take you away," Father continued. "If your...eccentricities continue...I will have the Brehons confirm your status, to match your mother's."

Confirm your status. I knew the Law. I'd ignored it for most of my life. It hadn't applied to me, I believed. My parents' union had been unique, undefinable. Father trained me as a druid since my birth. The Law was the Law. Father's status wasn't mine to inherit. My mother's status was. My mother was a servant, a slave. According to Law, so was I.

"If I'm a slave," I struggled against the knot in my throat, "how could I have begun the druid's training?" I meant to remain calm. I could pretend to have a reasonable conversation while inside I panicked with true fear.

"I raised you with my status because of your gift. We all saw it, even before you left Brocca's womb. You have proven yourself. I believe you should have a choice, of course. You've studied for many years on the druid path but now you have strayed from our teachings. This is the choice we will give you."

We. Maithghean must have prodded him. He used his one last threat.

"If you marry someone in the order, Tagdh, then you can continue your apprenticeship, and rise to a druid status. If not, your mother's status will apply."

This took me by surprise. I thought they would make me do the Test of the Ancients again. "Marry Tagdh , the bard? Why?"

"It's a reasonable match."

None of it made sense. Then I realized. They, the druid order of Fotharit, needed to watch me. I couldn't be forced into the Test. I wouldn't allow them into my thoughts. They wanted to control my memories as they returned. Take control of any power I could tap into. The Test of the Ancients wasn't over. Not at all.

"What if I don't want to marry Tagdh ?"

"If you refuse marriage to Tagdh , I will invoke the Brehons for a formal confirmation of your slave status."

I felt physically sick. "Would you have me be a slave in your home, like Mother?"

"Maithghean could probably use a servant's help more than me." Father's lip lifted as if in satisfaction, a grin quickly reigned in. I would be *Maithghean's* slave. To live in his house. To do as he bid. With my father's support. I should have gone with Mother.

I reached deep inside to find a calm face, calm words. A mask until I could figure out what to do. They couldn't control me with magic. They would control me with the Law.

"I'll consider your offer, Father." I had to make him believe this was my choice. Otherwise, they would take me again, test me again, all of the druids. They'd done it before. "Tagdh is a good man."

"So you will marry him?"

"It's better than slavery, isn't it?" Father couldn't expect me to be completely accepting of his threat.

"Now, Brigid."

I had to make it sound like I agreed that my druid apprenticeship was most important. I had to be compliant for a while. "And I can continue my studies. I can learn the healing arts with Elían?"

"As soon as you and Tagdh formalize your union at Beltane. Until then...no more traveling to the forests."

That new rule shook me. "Why can't I visit Niamh? She needs my help."

"You've been missing instructional time with Elían. You need to stay in touch. If needed, Maithghean and I will care for the forest folk."

Another veiled threat. They would hurt Niamh if I refused, they would find the healers who lived there. I would be watched until I married Tagdh, not allowed to leave the village. I couldn't give Father any idea that I would leave. I had to pretend to go along with his plan.

"Fine." I clutched at the quartz in my pocket, the stone Father had given me years ago that began my path, I wondered if it had any meaning left. "I will marry Tagdh, as long as you promise me that I can continue my apprenticeship, that I will become a full druid."

"I'm glad you agree, Brigid. Do this, and you will become part of our druid order."

That evening, I tried to convince Lomman and his family to leave with me. Mother's Christian group would accept them.

"It's too dangerous for you," said Lomman. "With all of us, my mother, my brothers and sisters, we would all slow you down."

"You don't have to stay here and keep serving Dunlang."

Una and Lomman glanced at each other. "We've made plans," Una finally said. "Ever since Brocca left..."

"In the spring," added Lomman. "You don't have time to wait, not after what I saw, Brigid. You can probably stay with your mother for a few days, but you know the druids will come looking for you there."

Una brought out a leather satchel and handed it to me. Inside were two wool blankets, dyed a dark blue. "It's a cold time to travel," she said. "I hope this will help."

"It's best to leave now," Lomman said. "In the darkness." The village gates were locked and guarded. "Dunlang's prize bull might have been left in the pasture alone," Lomman explained with a smile. "He might need to be brought to his pen." He'd left the bull out on purpose.

"You've already planned this?"

"When I went into your house last night, I saw danger. That was no ritual, at least it didn't look that way to me."

I thought of everything I had at Father's house. Herbs, medicines, my druid plaid. I had only what I wore, my old dress and blue cloak, thick leather shoes, and Una's satchel, in which she added bread and cheese.

Outside, yoked to a cart, was a pretty milk cow.

"Cows don't pull wagons-"

Lomman didn't leave time for my questions. "Get in." He pushed me close to the bench seat and covered me with blankets and hay. The cart lurched forward.

Warriors stopped him at the gate.

"It's Dunlang's prize bull, you see," said Lomman. "This cow is the only thing he'll follow. If I tie him to the back and she's in the front, I might be able to get him home."

"And the druid's daughter? She's staying with you?"

"She's with my mother," said Lomman. "Go to the house and check, if you want. More trouble than she's worth actually. I lost the bull because I helped her and the druid out of that house fire."

The gates unlatched. The wagon lurched out of the village. The cow, not used to the job, started and stopped until Lomann led her. After what seemed like hours, the cart stopped.

"We're beyond the hill. They won't see you here."

I pushed away the blankets. Lomman lit a torch and scanned the hillside for the missing bull. "Thank you Lomman. What if the warriors go to your mother's house?"

He shrugged. "It's not her fault if you hid in the cart? Or maybe you went to the druid grove? I doubt they'll look too hard, if at all." We heard hoofbeats and the bull appeared. "Go, Brigid. I'll take care of the animals."

I said goodbye to my friend and walked along the road in darkness.

I would miss my home. As the sun rose, I envisioned the morning - the smith hard at work, surrounded by heat and metal, women spinning wool in front of their houses or pounding wheat in the quern. At the granary, Lomman's mother would bade me hello...I said a silent goodbye to all I had ever known.

CHAPTER 26

Patrick

Patrick awoke beside the cold campfire, drenched in sweat. Dear Lord, what is happening to me? He had a dream. A woman. One of those dreams. He rubbed his eyes, trying to forget the scene in his head. He saw her copper colored hair and a flash of green eyes. In his dream, he had touched a smooth curve of skin and tasted her lips. This was the last thing he needed, an imaginary woman. Probably the result of all of Dathi's stories of Brigid. No more of this. He had to focus on the flock and return them to Milliuc's farm. The summer season turned to harvest.

Adjusting back into the house was difficult. He made room to sleep against the drafty thatched wall, trying not to take up Eamon's space. Hopefully, no more dreams of the Danann woman would torment him.

"Why doesn't Milliuc leave you in the pasture, lad?" Conall grumbled upon his return. Patrick shrugged. He's the one that had to get used to the crowded living quarters after another summer of solitude. He didn't know what Conall was complaining about. Maura served mutton stew and the boys crowded around him.

"It's good to see you, Patrick," she said.

"What's it like, all those months alone?" Nial asked eagerly.

"It's... it is lonely, Nial. I watch after the sheep mostly." He savored his stew.

"Did you pray to your stick-god?" asked Nial.

Liam must have told his brother about the cross. He noticed the boy's keen eyes were upon him and hoped he wasn't frightened of him any longer.

"Yes, sometimes. Talking to God is not so bad."

Nial giggled, finding the idea ridiculous.

Eamon and Conall joined him at the table and tore bread apart with their huge hands. They stared at Patrick, unsure what to make of him. They spent the summers sowing oats and barley, a man's job. Shepherding was something a boy could do.

"Heard you tried to leave again. Wasn't last year's beating enough?" Conall asked in his gruff way. "Or the year before that?"

Patrick shook his head. He was exhausted and overwhelmed and felt at odds with the others. Maura handed him another bowl of stew. He lifted the bowl and drank the stew with rapid gulps. He set the empty vessel down and grabbed for the freshly baked bread. He shoved warm chunks of it into his mouth.

"What do you do up on those hills?" Eamon pressed, picking up where Nial left off.

Patrick flushed with warmth, uncomfortable to be at the center of attention. "I guess I think a lot."

"About what? The sheep?" Conall ribbed Eamon.

"No. I'm tired of sheep," he answered, face still red, allowing the men their joke. "I was wondering about your stories. The legends about the Danann people? The Fomorians?"

"Who's been telling you about that foolishness?" Conall asked.

"No one," Patrick said. "I heard a storyteller, when I tried to go west a few months ago, that's all." He left Dathi out of it.

"Did you make it to the harbor?"

"No, there were only a few houses, not a fort. I thought I had escaped."

"There are a few farmers close to the shore," Conall said. "His men followed you again, didn't they?"

"It's a wonder they aren't the shepherds, instead of me."

"Don't worry about it. People from here to the coast are loyal to Milliuc. He paid them well for your capture."

Patrick wanted to get Conall back on topic. "Well, the stories I heard their druids tell gave me something to think about in the pasture. The old ones, they said, the ancient ones. What do you know about them?"

"Fairies, is all," Maura said. "The Danann are fairies, na daoine sí. They hide beneath the rocks and take healthy babies to change into their own."

"You've said that before. But what of the old gods? The ones who settled the island."

"There's Lugh of the Long Hand," said Conall.

"That's right," Eamon joined in. "Some say you can still see Lugh in the sunlight. The Fomorians though, some believe they're ancestors of all the Irish, and those before them, the Fir Bolg." He nudged Conall with his elbow. "Big hulking creatures, the Fir Bolg. Could be anyone's granddad."

"Only if you were born in a bloody bog!" Conall roared at Eamon, his face red with anger.

"Temperamental about your Fir Bolg blood, are you?" Eamon taunted. The two men threw ancient attacks at each other.

"What about the goddesses? Brigid?" Patrick interrupted their insults. He hoped they would see his interest as simple curiosity. "The stories I heard were very different from my Christian beliefs in Britannia. No goddesses, for one."

Eamon reached for another hunk of bread and slathered it with rich butter. He was a skinny man but he ate endlessly. "Brigid is considered the old goddess of poetry. So that storyteller you heard—his stories and songs would have been inspired by that goddess."

"Keening, laments, too," Eamon continued. "You know when you hear women wailing at a funeral? That's a thing started by Brigid, when she lost her son at Magh Tuiredh."

"A lament is what he means," Maura said. "Only women understand the lament for a lost child. Brigid brought it, along with the poetry."

"Tell me then, are these Danann fairies or are they gods? Do you worship these gods and goddesses? Is that who your druids pray to?" Patrick asked.

"I don't know what the druids do," Conall laughed. "They're secretive behind their cloaks, hiding in the groves, calling rain or sun. We appreciate nature, recognize the seasons and the tides, and we let the druids figure those things out. But is it how we find you praying in the middle of a stack of wool, holding your tied-together sticks? No, I'd say not."

"Didn't know I'd been praying so much," said Patrick. "It was nothing out of the ordinary at home." He didn't mention that he rarely prayed in Britannia. He'd taken God and belief for granted.

"You and those sticks!" Liam burst out. "You're talking to them like you're soft in the head!"

"Liam!" Maura admonished.

But Patrick only laughed. "I am soft in the head, boy. Milliuc's guards have kicked me in the head so many times that now I'll talk to anything. Even the fairies."

Conall finished his brown bread and butter and lay down on his blankets. Eamon soon followed, and Maura began putting her children down for the night. Patrick sat awake at the table, adjusting to the sounds of humanity again.

CHAPTER 27

Brigid

On the hill overlooking the bay, I performed sunrise salutations alone. I scanned the countryside. I needed plants that were sacred herbs. Some were necessary for healing, others were necessary for working spells. Maithghean would search for me once he realized I was gone. He'd use his mind, his soul, to try to connect with mine. He'd follow me on the road or check with villages to see where I stayed. I called on the powers surrounding me and spent much of my time in a meditative trance as I walked. A bit of herbal magic kept me heavily cloaked in the cold, persistent mists, hidden while I journeyed. I worked the spells of mist and trance upon myself for protection.

Nights were difficult. I avoided other tuaths, which would have offered a comfortable guest lodge. I didn't trust druids who might know Maithghean. I slept under the trees and burrowed in my wool blankets. It was early spring, still damp and cold. I followed my mother's directions to the coastal village with the beehive huts. Go to where the ciffs break. Along the shore, under the cliffs.

After days of traveling along the rocky shore, I found them. Rounded huts emerged from under the cliffs, like part of the landscape.

A short, stocky man in worn homespun garb greeted me warily. "Who are you?"

"I'm here for my mother, Brocca."

The man's stern face broke into a smile. "You must be Brigid. I'm Cormac." Seeing that I didn't recognize his name, he added. "Your uncle. Brocca is my sister."

Another man hiked down the cliffs and joined in the welcome. "I'm Erc. I sent your mother the message about our community. It's a miracle that families are brought together again here."

"Where is she? My mother?" I was overwhelmed. An uncle, a family I never knew.

Erc pointed to the hillside above the cliffs. "She's bringing the cows in from the pasture."

I saw her and waved. "Go on, go to her. We'll put your things in her house and get you settled."

I ran to Mother, meeting her halfway on the path that led the cows to a stone built cowshed. We hugged and laughed. She laughed. She was happy.

"I'm glad you came here Brigid, but why?"

She was so happy, smiling, leading the animals to their shelter. "I'll tell you later, Mother."

Her eyes darkened. "Maithghean?"

"And Father."

Though Erc seemed to be the leader of the scattering of roundhouses, he wasn't a chieftain. There was no chieftain. People tended to central gardens and animals in the center of the settlement. Erc told me later that men would hunt together on occasion, but they also herded their cattle, as a community.

Cormac's roundhouse was snug compared to our large house in Fotharit. It was comfortable and warm. Cormac's wife, Orla, brought us hot tea, the same fragrant chamomile that my mother often made. They had also been servants, abducted with my mother. They had created a small space for my mother, bedding covered with warm woolens.

"When the weather turns, we'll build Brocca her own house, and Brigid, you too, if you decide to stay," Cormac said.

"I won't be staying. It's not fair to put you all at risk."

"What risk?" asked Mother. "What happened?"

"Later," I stalled. "Tell me about our family in Alba," I changed the subject, still wary of sharing my plans. Anyway, I wanted to hear about my grandmother, the war chieftain.

"We have many stories, but it's been a long time since we've told them." Cormac smiled at my mother. "Our lives and our paths were uprooted. Your mother told you she was studying the druid path?"

"Yes, as am I," I replied. But Mother had been unable to finish her training. She lived vicariously through my father and me instead. And now, my training may be incomplete too.

Cormac and Orla glanced at each other, then at us. "We have found something new here, something that gives us hope." A sinking sensation filled me, and I knew what they were going to say before they spoke.

"Following the Christain path changed our lives. Under his guidance, Erc organized this tuath and brought people to it. He explained how we could ask for our freedom. Or just leave." He glanced at Orla. "We didn't have permission like your mother did. But Erc and the others here promised to protect us if anyone came looking." They glowed with happiness.

"In the end we will have life everlasting. We won't be subjugated to an Irish chieftain," Cormac explained. "Or the class system that keeps us in servitude. Our teaching here is based on equality. Palladius taught this. Christ would not agree to keep us enslaved."

"The Christians wants to end slavery now, for everyone," said Mother. This new belief offered something to the slaves that the native Irish never would. Freedom. Hope.

"You have your freedom now," I said. "You left Fotharit, for good. That doesn't mean you have to give up everything you believe. What about your druid studies?"

"I can't go back to studying a path that's subject to those Brehon rules, Brigid. I can't."

"I know," I said. I was threatened with slavery too, by Law. Yet I knew I needed to continue the druid path. "That's why I'm here." I held up my wrists so they could see the rope burns. Then I told her, Cormac, and Orla about the assault, the fire, the threat Father made and the Law that made it so.

I stayed with Mother overnight. We devised a plan. It was risky but possible. If I could find a tribe to adopt me, to allow me to continue my training, I could become a full druid and the threat of slavery would be compromised. It would be a challenge. I would have to learn a new tribe's histories, genealogies. My training time would most likely double. But if this worked, Fotharit couldn't enslave another tribe's druid in training - not without a battle. Especially one who had survived the Test of the Ancients?

Cormac offered to find a man from the village to accompany me as I traveled, but I refused.

"Are you sure?" my uncle asked. "Daylight doesn't mean protection."

"I'll be fine. I don't want you to have any trouble here." And I didn't know how to explain it, but I would. I had my herbs, my medicines, and knowledge. Something was growing stronger inside me. Memories of the past and of the old gods and goddesses. I needed to find the power within me, harness it, and unlock it for myself.

We decided that I should head west, on the forest road, far from Maithghean's coastal influence. Accompanied only by my thoughts and the brightness of the full moon, I slept under oaks again. Power thrummed from the earth, from the trees with immense roots. I meditated on my Danann memories, yearning to know the faces that were nameless. Macha, Dagda were regular visitors to my dreams. Perhaps the flashbacks would make more sense. I reached downward, through the earth to the Danann spirits, waiting. *Please send me a sign*. Let me know what to do. The oak leaves swayed in the wind, speaking. I wouldn't give up. The earth heard and sighed with a hush.I walked west, leaving the ocean and purple mountains behind.

As I traveled, I saw how lucky I had been, raised in a druid's house. Famine had struck hard, and starvation had assailed villages to the west. It was no wonder the cattle raids on our lands had increased. Small wattle and daub huts scattered the countryside. Crops looked meager and the sheep, thin. I traveled with dried venison and hard bread from my father's druid share. Yet, I reminded myself, right now I wasn't a druid. Legally, I was a slave. Father was willing to make me Maithghean's slave. I repeated this in my mind, unbelieving the truth. Maithghean, I would have expected. But not Father. As I traveled, I thought about Father, who had fallen far from the pedestal I'd kept him on. He'd never freed Mother. It was foolish to think he would treat me differently.

I walked west, deeper into forest land, skirted bogs, glad for my flint and quartz to start a fire when I grew cold. Erc had accompanied me to the next tribe nearest the beehive huts, and that I allowed. Not all clans were accepting of Erc and his strange Palladian ideas, I found, especially the ones that had lost several slaves to the new religion. Still, these druids didn't know Maithghean so I accepted their hospitality for a night.

I recited histories as I walked, collected plants as I traveled, practiced the ceremonies for sunrise, sunset, star alignment. I had been in the midst of training, with years ahead of me but there was so much I *knew*. After the Test of the Ancients, ritual knowledge seemed to settle within me just as it did with the herbal remedies that Elían questioned. I meditated on the Test and what it revealed...a past life, scenes I remembered, knowledge of the gods, and so many faces that I could not place. Maithghean thought I had power from this but most of the time I felt confused.

While druids in other tribes were happy to talk with me, no one had space for a new apprentice, certainly not a stranger who showed up unannounced. These positions were closely guarded, I knew. No one wanted a stranger from another tribe to interfere with their lineage and birth rights for the druid order. I didn't mention Maithghean or Father. The farther west I went, no one cared or had heard of them anyway. I simply said my mother had joined the Christians and I needed a new home. I never mentioned the Test of the Ancients.

It seemed I would have to walk the entire island if I had to, pushing through winter mist and fog. I would need to find a tuath to take me in, or return to Mother and the Christians. I couldn't give up. I couldn't let my druid path stal l...it was all I knew. I couldn't go to another land...Britannia, Rome itself...those ideas didn't even make sense to me. It was here I belonged. I went back to the test, to understand what the Ancients were trying to tell me. So much had been lost. Macha and Dagda were mostly in the realm of story, some of the gods and goddesses were revived at Imbolc or Lughnasadh, but understanding what they were, the power of the ancient ones had faded over millennia. That's what it is. I began to focus on that idea. The fading power of the Tuatha de Danann.

One morning, at sunrise, I approached the tuath of Foclut Forest. Druids stood on a hillside outside of the village, performing the sunrise ritual. The western sea was a glimmer from the top of the hillside. This was as far as I could go. I set down my satchel and joined them.

The druid closest to me opened his eyes and smiled as the ritual concluded. "Brigid? We've been waiting."

I jolted at the sound of my name. My immediate thought was: Maithghean found me. The old druid continued to smile. He was a seer. An actual seer with life after life of talent, not making half-cocked, politically-influenced predictions with throwing sticks, like my father.

"You know my name."

"I do. I felt you would be joining us. I just didn't know when."

I was a little disconcerted by the all-knowing druid but I couldn't think of a time when I had met a seer so honest.

"Dathi mentioned your arrival many times," said a black-haired priestess. I noted the gold torc she wore. She was the chief druid of this tribe. "We were never quite certain if he was looking forward to Imbolc or if an actual Brigid would arrive. You can stay in the guest lodge as long as you need."

"Thank you." I picked up my things and followed the trail of a half dozen druids into the village. Dathi led me to the guest lodge, a small, comfortable roundhouse near the gates of the fort. I unpacked my blanket, cloak, collected plants and a handful of quartzite and flint. I sat on the pallet, exhausted. I had been traveling for well over a moon cycle into two. When I rested, I could meditate more on Foclut Forest and get a sense of the druids and people here. Dathi knocked at the door.

"We'd like for you to join us for supper in Raven's lodge." He glanced at the table, noting the plants, gathered as I traveled, were laid out to dry properly. Then he spied the stones. He picked up the flint and quartz and struck them together. "So you know the properties of fire?"

"Of course," I replied. "The heat is internal to both stones. Only together can they create a spark."

"How long have you been studying?"

"Since childhood." I stopped myself from saying anything more. I wasn't ready to talk about Father or Fotharit or the Test of the Ancients.

"There's more, isn't there? You know much more than the basic properties of stone and fire." I picked up my cloak. The plain blue. "Have you no plaid?" asked Dathi.

"Isn't Raven waiting for us?"

Dathi smiled his genial grin again. "She is. She, and the others, will be asking similar questions about why you are here. I thought you'd like to tell me first."

"Why?"

"A feeling is all, Brigid. You were meant to be here."

That was positive and the truth was, I felt the same. When meeting Dathi, something clicked into place. "Then I will tell you the same story I have told the others. My mother left our village to join a Palladian community far from home. I could have stayed with her, of course, but I'm already years into my druid training. I don't want to give that up."

"Why didn't you stay in your tuath? I'm sure accommodations could have been made."

"No. None could."

"They will ask for proof of your training. A message from your chief druid? A plaid cloak showing your years of study?"

"I can show you my skills. That's all that should matter." I walked outside, eager for his questions to end and to meet with Raven and the rest. I had no doubt Dathi knew something about what I hid. I would tell him, and the others, when I could trust them.

CHAPTER 28

Patrick

T he seasons turned and bitter cold gave way to softening light. Patrick hunkered with the ewes in their pens, as several were ready to give birth soon. He spent the winter months culling ewes with defects, especially those whose milk was slow. Their lambs were small, underdeveloped. Milliuc was determined not to let poor offspring happen again and he'd shown Patrick how to select ewes for successful breeding.

They spent enough time with the ram this summer, he mused, recalling the lusty beast. Milliuc hoped for both an early and late breeding season. Patrick sighed at the man's greediness. It was double the work for him. By mid-winter, the first sets of ewes were ready to birth.

Patrick skimmed the blade over their bulging bellies and delicately handled the knife over their crotches, a procedure which helped the ewes in the birth process and allowed him to see when the lamb was ready to arrive. When he had first arrived, he had vomited while assisting in the first birth, and Liam and Milliuc teased him for his weak stomach. To see another living creature emerge from the sheep was more than he could handle.

Now he knew the flock well. He culled the sickest ones. He made sure the healthy ones stayed healthy. He knew which ewes would make good mothers. Two ewes had dropped, swinging bulges from their hips, and the animals danced away at the lightest touch. Confined to his own pen, the ram's job was done for the season.

He checked the animals for signs of prolapse. Patrick found he genuinely cared about the animals. The helpless sheep were not the cause of his incarceration.

One ewe laid down, nose up in the air. Patrick called her Julia, a reminder of a Roman name. There was another he called Bella, due to have her lambs soon too. He didn't name all the sheep, but he did try to tell the expectant ewes apart by staining their sides with a berry dye. It was necessary to know who had given birth successfully in the previous seasons.

Patrick watched anxiously. He had no help this time from Liam or NIal; he alone was in charge of the animals, with threats of punishment from Milliuc if something went wrong. Patrick resented the threat and knew he didn't even need to be there. Unless there was a significant problem, animals could give birth by themselves. How was it his fault if something went wrong? He rechecked his supplies—a knife for the umbilical cord and some rags for cleaning the newborn.

"Come on, Patrick!" Liam stuck his freckled face into the pen. "It won't be born for hours. You don't need to sit and watch the entire time."

"Yes, I do. Milliuc said he'd rip my head off if one of his prized ewes or her lambs died." Patrick settled himself, determined to wait it out.

"Well, it's time to eat. Mam has supper on the table. Eamon and Conall are famished from being in the fields all day."

"Don't wait for me," Patrick said. He wasn't leaving his post. He couldn't imagine what Milliuc might do if he found him away from the animals. "But you could bring me a dish of something," he called after the boy.

Patrick sat on the barn floor, his arms wrapped around his long legs. He rested his face on his knees and prayed again. Please, holy Christ, be with this animal in her hour of need. Let her lamb survive. He didn't know if he prayed more for himself or the ewe he called Julia. They were in this together.

"What are you doing, Patrick? Sleeping on the job already?" Nial ran in and set a bowl of stew at his feet.

"No, praying," he said, startled at the interruption.

"Again?" the child asked, incredulous.

"Yes. Sometimes it happens." He smiled at the small boy, who had Maura's soft brown eyes.

"Why?" Nial asked.

Even though he'd explained it over and over, Nial still didn't understand. "Because," Patrick explained much the same way as he'd done before. "God is someone to talk to. He listens to your troubles."

Nial giggled at his response. "You're funny, holy boy. I'll tell Dathi that you should be a druid."

Dathi had told Patrick that himself, although he said more than once that Patrick was too old to start now. *Should have been* was the phrase he used. Patrick also realized that no one knew about the time Dathi spent with him, telling him to recall some sort of past. The Tuatha de Danann. Brigid. "Well, I don't think the druid path is for me, and my father might prefer that I be a priest. But right now, I'm a shepherd and that is all."

Nial sang as he left: holy boy, holy boy, all the way back to the house. Patrick reddened at the innocent taunt, puzzled why his fellow servants didn't understand prayer. He recalled the druid ceremonies he'd witnessed. Wasn't their ritual like prayer, the chants, the druids, the fires, spun to the people like a magnificent liturgy? Didn't they pray, individually, to their gods? The druids prayed to Nature herself, the wind, the sun. Occasionally, they threw in a sacrifice of a defenseless animal for good measure. Dathi said he needed to remember Brigid so the old gods could become the focus again. Patrick racked his mind trying to figure out how he was supposed to influence that change. His conversation with Conall and the others showed they weren't particularly interested in any kind of change.

He wiped his hand across his brow. The ewes did all the work, but it was Milliuc's threat that drained him. The guards had beaten Patrick enough to know he wasn't strong enough to handle another punishment. He was thin, malnourished. The food he received on the farm in winter couldn't make up for his paltry meals in the summer. He existed on what grains Milliuc left for him and whatever bread Dathi brought him; salmon he could catch, and occasional greens. It was a feast if he brought down a rabbit with his sling, but there was a serious lack of fat in his summer diet.

The ewe bleated. It was Julia's first birth and panic showed in her eyes. Another contraction went through her and she made another noise. Patrick patted her head and ran his hand gently over her bulging stomach. She quieted and seemed to let instinct override her fears. Hours passed. Julia was fading, tired. She lay on her side, unwilling to push any more. Milliuc's warning haunted Patrick. He would be severely punished if the lamb or ewe died. He supposed he would be beaten again—not a prospect he looked forward to, even though he knew now how to protect himself from the harshest blows. The only reason Milliuc didn't get rid of him altogether was because of Dathi. Well, Dathi should be here now helping him with the sheep.

He pushed the ewe to a standing position and made her walk around the small enclosure. Exercise. It helps the lamb fall out. The poor mother-to-be-walked in circles, anxious to have her ordeal ended. She returned to her resting place, and Patrick checked her progress. Something showed through the opening. A tail, a little lamb's tail. Wait a minute. That's not right. Julia *baaed* in frustration. He couldn't do a breech by himself. He'd need help.

Patrick ran to the house to ask Liam. They were all asleep.

"Liam," he shook the boy urgently. "Wake up. I need your help!"

"G'way." The young boy rolled over, exhausted. He did a man's work these days. He cut wood and repaired stone walls. He was probably in no mood to get up and do a job that wasn't his.

"Liam." Patrick shook him again, panic growing with each passing second.

"Wha—?" Liam rubbed his eyes and gave the frantic young man an angry look.

"Please help. The lamb is backwards. I don't know what to do." He didn't want either animal to die, and he also didn't want to be beaten within an inch of his life. Again.

"Pull it out." Liam turned back over, his face in his blanket.

"What? Pull it out? How?"

Liam sat up and glared at him. "Reach in and pull it out by the arse or legs or whatever you can get a hold of. Now leave me alone, holy boy."

Patrick stood in the dark, stunned and hurt by the boy's rejection. Liam used to idolize him and used to eagerly help him. He was older now, looking for the approval of Conall.

Patrick ran back to the barn and prayed that the ewe and her half-born lamb were still alive.

"Dear Lord, help me. Please let these animals live." Desperate and alone, he was overwhelmed with responsibility. Cold panic settled in the pit of his stomach.

Then he remembered what Dathi had taught him about this season. Imbolc. Brigid's holiday. Fine. He'd ask for help from one of the Irish goddesses too. "Brigid. Anyone."

Julia breathed hard, eyes wild with pain. He checked the positioning of the lamb again and saw the full tail of the baby. No, that was all wrong. He took a deep breath and sent out another mental call for help from whatever gods listened. He lifted the ewe's rump and reached in, beneath the backwards lamb. The womb squeezed his arm like a vice. He felt around, searching for the legs.

Something...someone was helping him, guiding him on what to do.

That's the nose, so his legs should be nearby. Patrick grasped a small hoof and turned the small body as gently as he could. *Work with her contractions, bring each hoof into the birth canal.* Finally, the front legs protruded as they should. *Pull down, not out, follow the direction of the birth canal.* The lamb came forward.

The poor ewe was exhausted. He wiped the mucus from the baby's nose and cut the umbilical cord with the dulled knife. He set the newborn next to the mother, and she licked her clean.

"Thank you," he whispered to the voice, and fell asleep against the wall of the pen.

CHAPTER 29

Brigid

I worked with Raven on herbalism and healing, and Dathi on prophecy. The bards didn't know what to do with me. When it came time to repeat their histories, I knew. I could describe their ancestors, their generations of warriors, of druids. If I tried, I knew their songs. I knew Fotharit's too. It was as if every day, new knowledge seeped into me, quiet and unobtrusive.

"Here." Raven pointed me to a patch of burdock. "What do you use this for?"

"It detoxifies, it's a mild painkiller. Some people can't tolerate willowbark. It upsets their stomachs. I'd use burdock instead."

"That's it?"

"If a warrior has an infected wound, I'd make tea from it. It helps for the pain, but also sends the poisons from his body."

And so on. We'd find a new plant and review the process. Raven didn't have to teach me anything new.

When I met with Dathi, we'd walk to a quiet hill outside of the village and meditate for hours. We'd open our eyes and Dathi would simply wait for me to tell him what I saw, if I told him anything at all. Even more, as we met day after day, I felt a kinship with him, a bond. "Soul friends?" I asked after one of our meditations.

"I think so. You would have to tell me more. I think your knowledge of it is stronger than mine." He waited for me to tell him more.

"There's a reason why I know these things." I waved my hand toward the tuath below. "The plants, the bardcraft..." I had no guarantee that Dathi and Raven and the rest wouldn't be like Maithghean and want to take everything from me. Dathi sensed that.

"We won't hurt you here. We have a different philosophy than most. Maybe it's because we're isolated from so many tribes here in the west. We revere the ancients, not the clan chiefs or the warriors."

"I've seen that in my few weeks here...it's about the Test of the Ancients." He waited expectantly and I continued. "I've been subjected to it."

"And you survived. Well, obviously." Dathi closed his eyes, as if he spent a moment in silent meditation. "I knew you had gifts, Brigid, and thought there would be a past life involved..."

"I can't answer all of your questions." I cut him off there. The mention of the past made me cringe. I wasn't ready to deal with all of it. "But I passed the test. Sometimes memories come to me. Sometimes it's only impressions, feelings. Sometimes I just know things, like this, the druid work. No one taught me bardcraft. I just knew."

"If you survived the test, it means the Old Ones protect you. It means...it may mean a lot of things." He left unsaid the obvious purpose and consequences of the test: I had recalled a past life as an ancient one. "Our goal here is to bring back the old ones across this land," he said finally. "Our people are no longer united. We fight, we raid for cattle, we enslave our prisoners of war...if we bring back the ancient ones, those things may change."

This was the first time I'd heard anyone question the battles and the raids. "How? Most of the tuaths keep the ceremonies and raids continue." I thought of Dunlang's summer battles, encouraged by Maithghean, always for more cattle, more land, more slaves.

"You know it is more than the ceremonies. It's as if when the Danann left, they took the magic with them and now all we do is raid for cattle and fight over chieftains."

We walked to another hillside that overlooked the farmlands to the edge of the western sea. I'd never thought I would travel this far to see the other ocean so far from the bay of my youth.

"What it will take," said Dathi, "is a rejuvenation of belief. People need to feel that the ancient ones are with them. It's a presence they seek, not more ritual." I began to understand what Dathi was asking for. I needed to reveal the truth about the Test of the Ancients and work on the memories the test had unlocked. "It will take time. You don't need druid training, Brigid, to need to work with what you already possess."

"But I can't be called a full druid without finishing an apprenticeship."

"The path set before you is broader than being a druid in a local tuath, isn't it? Think about it, Brigid. Meditate on it. Few survive the Test of the Ancients. The path given to you from that test runs beyond one village. Would being a healer here or in your own tuath be enough?"

My mind reeled and I didn't know where to begin. I had been so focused on my druid training, particularly to keep the threat of slavery away, that I hadn't thought about any other options. There weren't any other options, not formally, not ones recognized by Law, druid, or tribe.

"There are people you need to meet." Dathi gestured to the farmland below.

"Farmers?"

"Some. Also servants, children, slaves. They are the ones who we need to work with. Not druids. Not chieftains. The people, all of them. Talk to them. Share with them Brigid's story, Brigid of the Tuatha dé Danann. Brigid. *Remember.*"

Imbolc. My namesake day. My day - if the Test of the Ancients was true. Of course it was true. I knew it to be so. Dathi and Raven argued whether I should have a part in the Imbolc ceremony.

"If we allow her this," said Raven, "what will the village think? We haven't adopted her. We haven't apprenticed her."

You should, I thought to myself and Raven gave me a quick glance. I wondered how loudly my thoughts traveled.

"Think of it as a test of her skills," said Dathi.

"We know her skills."

They argued in front of me in the guest lodge, away from the other druids. At the moment, I didn't care what they decided. The few weeks in their guest lodge at the edge of the western sea gave me more peace than I had ever known. For the first time in my life, I was free of Maithghean. I slept well. I dreamt of the Danann, the amber-eyed man, the shepherd but as continuing dreams, not the nightmares of my childhood.

"You know she is beyond apprenticeship," Dathi continued. I returned to their conversation.

"What do we do for this ceremony?" asked Raven. "How do we introduce her to the tribe?"

"Simply as Brigid. It's Imbolc. It would be fitting."

Raven scoffed. "Are we telling our people she is the goddess personified? This isn't a child's game, Dathi. We can't bring up the Test of the Ancients to the entire tribe."

I wanted to be part of the ritual. I had performed the chants alone as I traveled. Only me, the bonfire, the stars. I wanted to be part of a druid order but I understood Raven's misgivings. My presence complicated the traditional ceremony.

"I've explained to you the purpose," said Dathi. He'd explained it to Raven but not to me.

Finally, Raven relented. "We'll say she is a guest and leave it at that."

I nodded my agreement although I felt the same chord of panic since leaving Fotharit. If I wasn't accepted into a druid order, I could be remanded as a servant.

"Let's walk," said Dathi, his usual request to speak privately, away from the tuath, on the hill that overlooked the farms below and the sea to the west. Ewes with their newborn lambs dotted the landscape. New light, new life, new lambs were the reason for Imbolc, symbols of our survival.

"We've created a part in the ceremony for you, where we can harness the Test of the Ancients," said Dathi. I wrapped my blue cloak around me, against the winter chill. I had asked Raven if I could weave a plaid. No, she'd said. Not until my status was formalized. Perhaps this was a step in the right direction, a part in the Imbolc ritual. "I believe, and Raven agrees, there is someone here, a connection if you will…"

"A connection?"

"I can't say more. I have only an impression, a guess. You will have to draw on what you know and who you recognize. We are asking you to point them out, to use your powers to find another to help you…when that happens, you will give this person a token, a lamb, perhaps. Fitting for Imbolc." His voice trailed off.

"I'm supposed to recognize someone and give them a lamb? How?"

"Only you have that power of recognition."

"What if I don't?" I knew the answer to that question. My apprenticeship was at stake. Being named a full druid was at stake.

Dathi swept his arm toward the green hills, the farms, the sea. "We believe there is another who will help you change this land. Another who will help you accomplish the goals of our tribe, to bring the Ancient Ones back to Éire."

CHAPTER 30

Patrick

P atrick worried about Julia over the following weeks. Her newborn lamb thrived, but she was listless, not recovering from the difficult birth as she should.

Milliuc gathered everyone to the sheep pen to announce that they would attend Imbolc ceremonies in the ring fort, as they did for all the high holidays. "It's the lambing season. I want the druids to bless our animals for a powerful flock." Milliuc noticed the ailing ewe and glared at Patrick. "What happened? Why is she down?"

Patrick hadn't told him about the breech birth. Milliuc hadn't asked, either. Patrick didn't feel it necessary to say anything. He didn't want to incur the man's wrath if it wasn't necessary.

"I don't know. She had a difficult time at the birth…" His voice trailed off as Milliuc's blood boiled to his face; the fair roots of his mustache speckled against the vibrant red of his skin. Patrick cringed and wished he had killed him with the shearing knife.

"I warned you that all was to go well! She was a first-time ewe! She should last for many birthing seasons!" He grabbed Patrick by the neck of his tunic. "We will go to Imbolc so my flock will be blessed. If anything happens to my animals, you will face the consequences." Milliuc stomped out of the lambing pens. Patrick trembled. Conall and Eamon looked away, and even Nial refused to meet his eye. The threat was real.

The servants finished the morning chores and walked to the ring fort to join the celebration. Other households followed the road into the village, and a bustling, light-hearted energy surrounded them. Liam and Nial ran ahead, and Maura seemed happy for the change of scenery. Eamon, excited to meet a woman he had his eye on from the Samhain festival, bounded along with the younger boys.

"Go on," Conall called.

Patrick dragged his feet, brooding over Milliuc's threats. What was he supposed to do? He wasn't an expert with animals, even after all this time. He had never presided over the births alone, like some sort of midwife.

Maura walked beside him. "It's a wonderful day, isn't it?"

"How is it wonderful, Maura?" His mind was still stuck on his probable beating. "We're servants. We're trapped! How can you possibly be happy?"

She stopped and faced him. Her gentle eyes grew hard. "What use is it to sulk around every day? I try to take each day as it comes and enjoy what I can; the sun shines, my boys are happy, and a festival to enjoy with no work for a day. Don't disparage me because of it."

Patrick knew in his heart she was right, but he couldn't accept his condition, festival or no.

"I like Imbolc," Maura walked on. "It's not like Samhain." She's trying to cheer me up, Patrick thought. His temper had flared again. He didn't need Liam and Maura both angry with him.

"No, I don't. That ceremony is a little too dark for me."

"The sun is shining through the clouds today," Maura said contentedly to Patrick as they walked. "It's a wonderful day to celebrate the coming of spring. We'll have more daylight too. That's another gift from Brigid, the light. Poetry, lambs, light. Brigid's festival."

He knew the reason for Imbolc. He definitely preferred it over Samhain, although he kept to the wall of the fort with the gods for any ceremony. This one, though, was hopeful, rituals for the new lambs, and to celebrate the goddess Brigid, as Dathi had explained. Brigid again. The name unnerved him.

Conall joined them and took Maura's hand in his. Patrick noticed the gesture with surprise. When did this happen? Has everyone paired off but me? He nodded a greeting to Conall, who nodded back coolly. There was something between them, a difference of rank and duty. Patrick, as a shepherd, would always be the lowest of the farmhands.

The druids circled clockwise, the way of the sun. Patrick recalled Imbolc festivals in years past not quite understanding. He had to admit that now, he found the ritual fascinating, given that his biggest concern was the health of a nursing ewe. The druids and the people chanted, invoked Brigid's name, and circled the fire again. *Brigid.* Recognition. *She* was there. Somehow.

The circular movements of the crowd grew faster, and he saw a whirl of color swell from the center of the white robed druids. Maura grabbed his hand and pulled him into the dance. The colorful energy expanded outward. The crowd intensified the rotational chant, moving faster, begging Brigid for sunlight and for the start of spring.

Patrick sensed a presence...the ritual had worked. He felt a small murmur in his head, a pull on his heart. He looked around wildly in the crowd. He continued the spiral dance and held hands with Maura and Nial. He craned his neck, skimming the faces in search of whatever it was that beckoned to him. The presence enveloped the air around him. The whirling dancers continued wrapped in the colorful cloak of magic they created with their chants. He spun, wove, and danced, eager to touch what whispered past.

Then, the dance slowed. Druids formed an inner circle as the people gathered around them. One of the young priestesses held a small bleating animal high in the air. Patrick realized it was a newborn lamb. *Please, please don't sacrifice it.*

"Bless our flocks," Dathi called. "Brigid, *breo-saigit,* goddess of light and of fire, bring the light of spring to us." The priestess repeated Dathi's chants. A chill ran down Patrick' spine to hear Brigid's name spoken in ritual. Were they going to sacrifice that small lamb to her? Brigid cared for the animals, according to Dathi's stories. She wouldn't want them dead for no reason. He wouldn't let an animal sacrifice happen, whoever this woman was. A flash of memory .... he was in the fields, a copper-haired woman was with him, they herded the sheep back...back to where? Where were they? When?

"We cherish the new life of the coming spring. Let the lambs thrive on their mother's milk." She held the lamb high for all to see.

I'll reach in and pull the lamb out of the flames if this horrid druid drops her in the fire. He pushed to the front of the crowd. The priestess circled the lamb in the air once more as the other druids chanted incantations for good health and ewe's milk. The tiny animal *baaed* as the druidess held her again to the sky. Then, swiftly, she brought the lamb down low so that the wool brushed the flames.

Then she stopped short from dropping the animal in. She walked around the fire and handed the lamb to Patrick.

"Here, shepherd, another lamb for your flock. This will be the first of many to follow you." Her voice was quiet, meant just for him. And familiar. Patrick recognized her voice.

Patrick took the animal in his arms while the crowd gasped around him. He stood stunned, unsure of what to do, while he held the bleating lamb. He looked into the eyes of the druidess again and found recognition. Her green eyes, her copper hair. He knew her in a way that settled into the depths of his soul.

CHAPTER 31

Patrick

Julia, the sick ewe, died the following morning. The difficult breech birth had caused too much damage to her internal organs and infection set in. Patrick sat next to her in the pen, stunned. Hadn't the druids blessed this flock? Didn't the druids give him the sacrificial lamb? Julia's newborn nosed her gently. He would have to graft this lamb, along with the druid's gift, onto Bella and hope that the ewe would adopt both orphaned lambs.

Patrick rubbed his eyes. Lambing season was different from the sheep they chose for slaughter each year, the ones that made up his nightly mutton stew. He had cared for Julia, went through the struggle of her birth...Brigid even helped him. Or had she? He didn't know what was real anymore. His mind spun from his participation in the Imbolc ritual.

Milliuc's footsteps thudded into the lambing shed. Patrick had forgotten about the promised punishment due to the excitement of the Imbolc ceremony. He steeled himself for heavy fists. The farmer entered the pen alone, without his two guards who always did the dirty work; Milliuc never struck Patrick himself.

When Milliuc entered, Patrick decided to stand. No more cowering at his feet. If Milliuc was going to beat him, then let him do it, but Patrick would no longer accept the punishment.

He surpassed Milliuc in height by an easy six inches. Patrick was thin, but his muscles had hardened to his tasks, and he no longer feared the stout, barrel-shaped man. Milliuc observed the dead ewe. Patrick knew it wasn't the first time one died in labor, and it certainly wouldn't be the last. *Go ahead.* His eyes bore into Milliuc's dull gray ones. *I should have killed you long ago, when I had the chance.*

The shorter man flushed red, as if Patrick had spoken his thoughts. Milliuc clenched his meaty fists but kept them at his side.

"I warned you," he said, voice tight and controlled.

Patrick said nothing. If Milliuc wasn't going to hit him, what would he do?

"You will stay in this pen until you take the animals to pasture on the next moon. Maura will bring you meals and that is all. You won't speak to any member of this household unless they're sent here by me." He huffed a little at the end of his pronouncement, as if proud he had thought of it so quickly.

A solitary life during the summer was enough. But permanent isolation in the lambing shed? Patrick regretted his previously selfish thoughts. When he first arrived, he had looked down his nose at the state of the servants hut, the crowdedness, and the fact he –the son of a decuriones—had slept in the same room as slaves. Suddenly, he cherished every moment of human contact. Patrick gained control over the shocked expression on his face. He wouldn't let Milliuc know he had won.

The remnants of an intolerably slow winter passed with heavy frosts and soggy rains. In the shed with the lambs, Patrick edged close to the realm of madness. He believed that Milliuc would relent after a few days. He couldn't possibly stay in the animal pens before they moved to pasture. But he did.

The pens were filthy, even though Patrick's job was to clean them daily. Moldy straw covered the ground, loosely decorated with the black pellet droppings from the animals. Although he replaced the straw daily as best he could, it didn't take long for the dozens of animals to dirty it up again.

Wind howled cold through the half-covered shed, a semi-shelter built for sheep. Only the pregnant ewes stayed in the enclosed barn. Shivering, Patrick dug out a corner for himself next to one of the sheep, burrowing close to the wooly animal for warmth. He was used to sleeping outside, and he was used to isolation, but not in the last weeks of winter. On his first night in the pens, he looked out over the farm. Firelight flickered from the two houses across the field. Surely, Maura would let him in for the night or give him a blanket. Patrick crept to the edge of the pen as the lambs *baaed* with his movement.

"You stay in the pens!" Milliuc was there, a dark shadow at the edge of the sheep's pens. Patrick stopped, unbelieving that the landlord would spend the night outside to guard him. Patrick crawled back into the pen, curling up next to Bella.

The sun edged over the horizon, breaking light into the tortuous night. Numbly, Patrick awoke from one of the smattering pockets of sleep that caught him for brief moments. His bladder ached and he stepped out of the pen to relieve himself in the trenches at the edge of the yard. Milliuc appeared, shoving him hard back onto the straw.

"I'm going to..." Patrick pointed as Conall stumbled out of the servants' house to the trenches.

"You—stay—in—the—pens," Milliuc growled, punctuating each word as if Patrick were just learning the language. Two warriors grinned behind him and all three men towered over the young man sitting in the straw.

"Stay? What about...?" His eyes darted toward the area his painful bladder most desperately needed.

Milliuc shrugged. "I'm sure the sheep here will show you to their facilities."

Patrick watched from a crack in the corner of the shed as Liam and Conall worked in the fields clearing stones, making room for expanding crops. Liam was growing into a young man, Patrick observed, acutely missing their friendship from the previous year. He saw Eamon return from visiting his woman in the village every few days, jubilant. How does he get permission to leave? Patrick wondered. Why does Milliuc hate me so much? Aside from his constant escape attempts. Aside from Dathi's blatant favoritism.

After the first three days, the guards left. Patrick didn't know if they had gone on an errand for Milliuc or if they would return at all. They hadn't spoken to him, only glowering over the edge of the pen if he dared to near it. When they didn't return after dark, Patrick took the chance. He ran to the servants' house, hoping for a short respite from his isolation.

Conall blocked the door. "You're not coming in," he whispered fiercely, allowing his bulk to fill the doorway.

"Why not?" Patrick searched for an opening between Conall's muscular body and the door.

"Look, lad, the druids took some kind of favor on you and it angered Milliuc. We don't want any part of it."

"But I didn't do anything! Please, let me come in for tonight to keep warm. I'll leave before the sun rises."

Conall shook his head and closed the door. Patrick slumped against it, humiliated beyond words. He returned to the pen. He thought about escaping again. Then he heard the laughter of men in the distance, guards at the boundaries of Milliuc's fence. He couldn't leave now. Besides, he had no supplies or food. His booley hut in the pasture was better stocked with provisions.

Shivering in the sheeps' pen, he threw handfuls of straw over himself and found his place in the huddle of ewes. The smell of dank wool assaulted him, a bleak reminder of the sack placed over his head at his kidnapping. Bella, protective of her adopted newborns, snapped her teeth at him when he came too close.

Lord, please help me, he began. Never mind. You don't care, do you? I gave you no reason to care. I didn't believe in Britannia, despite my grandfather's efforts to direct his homily to me at church. Is that why, God? Is that why you have left me now?

The only sound was a soft *baa* of a lamb.

He closed his eyes, hoping for sleep. The priestess from the festival invaded his dreams with a sparkle of green eyes and a flash of copper hair. He knew the scent of her when it wafted through the air. *Where are you?* He called.

I'm trying. She spoke as if at the other end of a tunnel, a hollow echo.

Patrick awoke, startled. sat up. Trying? Where are you? He felt her panic. He stood, searching with a sense of urgency. This is ridiculous. You believe that you are talking to this woman from the heathen ceremony. He sat back next to Bella, who bleated at him in annoyance.

Milliuc sent Patrick from the farm when the first shoots of green poked through the damp soil. Patrick breathed a sigh of relief as he left the boundaries of the sheep pens. Now, the loneliness reached him as he camped beneath newly-budded trees, while he followed the growing flock of sheep over the hillsides of Milliuc's tribal land.

His loneliness didn't last long. Dathi appeared over the hillside with the young priestess. Brigid. He already knew her name.

CHAPTER 32

Brigid

"It's time," said Dathi. "You chose the shepherd."

"I recognized him," I said. "It wasn't a matter of choice." Another door opened because of the Test of the Ancients. I knew that man. I had seen him in my dreams all my life. I saw him during the Test of the Ancients. The shock was real at the Imbolc ceremony. I jolted as if hit by lightning. I *knew* him. But I had a part to play before the druids. And I had to give him the lamb.

When we approached him in the pastures, he didn't appear to recognize me or care at all that we were there. He was supposed to help us with the Ancient Ones, to share the stories. Maybe the servants would follow our past again, instead of the Pallidans on the eastern coast. Dathi told me he had prepared him for moons and had taught him the bardcraft.

"Remember, Patrick, the Ancient Ones? I told you the stories about the Danann and the Lia Fail."

"I remember." He held on to his walking staff and looked beyond us to the sheep in the pasture.

"Now it's time," said Dathi. "You and Brigid will work together to share those stories with the people."

Patrick looked at me and shrugged. "Fine. I've nothing else to do."

I looked at Dathi. "I don't think he's prepared for this."

Dathi smiled. "Just wait."

Dathi brought us together to practice meditations, to work on memories of the past, our lives before this one. Patrick and I sat before him, eyes closed while he chanted ancient words and ancient verse. I felt glimmerings, vague impressions while Patrick sighed and shifted in his cross-legged seat. After several days of hiking out to the shepherd's booley hut, I'd had enough.

"Dathi. Stop," I said. His chants ceased. "We can't do this on command."

"Whatever this is," added Patrick.

Dathi sat next to us, weary. "I have seen it. Both of you, together, help to heal this land. All you have to do is -"

"Remember," said Patrick. He stood, stretching his long legs. He gazed into the distance, keeping track of the sheep.

I'd wondered about his negativity the first few days of the meditation practice. "Why are you doing this?" I asked earlier. "You clearly don't want to."

"You and Dathi came to me, remember? You handed me a lamb. As far as I'm concerned, you are someone to talk to."

I did give him the lamb at Imbolc. As the druids chanted the magic and the people danced around the bonfire, I saw him. Patrick. There, but reluctant. It was him. I'd seen him in dreams, the shepherd with his staff.

"Brigid," Dathi asked. "Did you have any memories? Anything new today?"

"I don't think this can be forced, Dathi. You're trying too hard," I said. "And Patrick could get into a lot of trouble if Milliuc found out. This is dangerous for him."

"I can handle Milliuc," said Dathi.

"I can't," said Patrick bitterly. "I'm the one who gets beaten if a sheep is lost. I was locked in a lambing shed all winter. You show up after the fact."

This is why meditations didn't work. Too much worry. Dathi closed his eyes. He didn't want to relinquish control of his experiment.

"I need to be alone to meditate. Maybe Patrick does too." Patrick's eye caught mine with the slightest raised eyebrow. It was the first time I'd seen any lightheartedness from him.

"That may be best," said Dathi. "Except he can't be alone - he doesn't know what he's doing."

That earned another raised brow from Patrick. "I've been alone up here for years," he said. "I haven't experienced any amazing memories."

"Maybe not," said Dathi. "But you perfected an entire language in a few days listening to raiders on a boat." Patrick turned away. Dathi hadn't told me about this. I would have to ask Patrick about it later. Dathi continued with his instructions. "You two alone here might work."

"Perhaps less structured meditation," I suggested. "More dream work. He's not a druid. Let whatever he recalls appear naturally."

"And Milliuc?" asked Patrick.

"I've told him I'll watch you and to leave the guards at the road," said Dathi.

I felt awful. While Dathi and I were talking about druid methods, I forgot that Patrick was a slave. He wasn't here because he *wanted* to be. He was forced here. He'd been kidnapped, a practice we wanted to stop. His clothes were threadbare. He wore a dirty woven shirt, some kind of similar breeches. He said he'd been trapped in a barn and it showed. Dathi had brought a basket of food, as he usually did, but a loaf of bread and a few apples might only last Patrick a day or two. He needed more food, warm clothing, and medicines. Dathi seemed so intent on his vision that he didn't see that Patrick was suffering right in front of him.

I broached the subject carefully as Dathi and I returned to the guest lodge. "Let me work with him alone," I said. "He's used to resisting you."

"You can try, Brigid. I know he has great talent. He is key for helping us with our mission."

"He's also been a slave for years. It's going to take time. Will Raven allow me to stay in the pastures with him?"

"I'll discuss it with her."

"Dathi," I said as he turned to leave. "Wait. What about my training?"

"I'll talk to Raven again. If you succeed with Patrick, I think we can make your druid status official."

I smoothed out my wool cloak. Dathi had taken me in, allowed me to participate. But I had no druid plaid. "My status is dependent on the shepherd? No matter what?"

"No...no, of course not. Raven and I will come up with something. I promise. It won't be a traditional acolyte ceremony. It will have to be something new."

In the morning, I gathered my satchel and baskets. I searched around the guest lodge for bread, cheese, blankets, and medicines.I walked through the forest, up the hillside, to the booley hut. Patrick wasn't there. I set my bags down, confused. I wondered if I was lost. This was the place we had met, above the river, between the two oaks. In the distance, toward the sea, there was a flock of sheep. Of course. He had to move the flock. I followed the sheep's path westward. The land opened up into a continuously rolling hillside, the view of the western sea opening up with each crest.

Half a day later, I found Patrick, staff at his side, inspecting a ewe's hoof.

"Is she hurt?" I asked.

"Just a stone bruise, I think." He sent the sheep on her way and turned to greet me. "I saw you coming" He pointed to the rolling hills and the sheep's path. He noted my bags. "Set them there." He had his own blanket and belongings in a pile. A meager little.

"Where's the booley hut?" I asked.

"None here. I like to take the sheep here if the weather holds and camp a few nights before returning to the hut."

Patrick emptied the basket and found the wool tunic I'd been knitting for him. He pulled off his old shirt. His ribs were visible, each one. His pelvic bones stuck out sharply. Dathi had been telling me about Patrick, how I had to meet him, how we had to work together. Yet Dathi never mentioned that Patrick was the poorest slave I'd seen. My mother was in bondage but lived in a druid's house. Lomman's family still had the shelter of the tuath and the chieftain's lodge.

"You can rationalize it all you want," said Patrick. "Slavery here is an evil, whether me on these hills, the farm workers, or household servants."

"You knew my thoughts? All we needed was for Dathi to go away for a while?"

He rolled his eyes. "The look on your face for one. You made me new clothes, for another. I'm not a mind reader."

I waited until he'd emptied the basket. "There's more here." I handed him my satchel. "Extra cheese, dried venison. I took it from the druid's storage."

"I wonder why Dathi never brought me meat." He chewed on a strip, hungry for protein.

"I don't think he thought about it. He rarely eats meat. He says it interferes with his seer work."

Patrick shook his head like that was the most ridiculous thing he'd ever heard. "Must be nice to have the luxury of choosing not to eat."

"So." He gestured to the grazing sheep and climbed up on a boulder. "This is one of my favorite places to watch them."

"Should we practice without Dathi?" I felt suddenly awkward.

"You can do whatever you want. My job is here." He nodded toward the sheep again.

"But...the memories. The Tuatha dé Danann."

"I'm only doing all of that because Dathi is close to Milliuc. He watches me. I can't disobey Dathi. I'm sure he's told you I'm a Christian. Your stories are interesting but it's not anything I *believe*."

"Dathi isn't watching you. He's been protecting you."

"Brigid, all I want to do is leave. If he wanted to protect me, he'd show me the path to a nice harbor, with a nice ship, that would take me back to Britannia. All I've done is walk in circles since I got here."

I folded the blankets and organized the food he'd dumped on the ground. I knew exactly where the harbor was, with the ships. It wasn't too far from Mother, from the Palladians. I climbed up next to him on the boulder. "I can tell you."

I'd never seen him so hopeful. He smiled. He actually smiled. "Brigid. Where?" He pointed east. "I follow that road there and then -"

"No, that road turns south and then back to the forest. You need to stay south then find the eastern road through the bogs -" There it was, a flash of memory, so bold and strong, I grew dizzy. An image of us, of Patrick and I together on a boulder.

"Brigid, are you all right?" He held my shoulders to keep me from falling.

The world spun and I couldn't tell if his voice was from the present or the past. I held tight to his forearms, hoping he shared in this vision. We were together, a field, sheep, a house...but so long ago. Here, but not here.

"Take this." He handed me his water bag but I couldn't drink. Everything spun around me. "Are you sick?"

"This is what happens with the memories." Mother had been right about the effects of the Test of the Ancients. The memories were intense. If I were in Fotharit, Maithghean could have taken advantage of my weakened state.

Patrick slid down from the rock and set out his blanket. He motioned me to it and I followed. He built a fire with the quartz and flint I'd brought and heated water for tea. I held my head in my hands until my mind began to still.

"I'll help you," I said finally. "I can give you a map to the harbor, but please stay until we understand this, these visions."

"You know where to go?"

"I came here from the east. There are harbors, many of them but the one you want is near my mother. She lives with a community of people who believe as you do."

He handed me the tea and I wrapped my hands around the earthenware cup. "Your mother is a Christian?"

I took a sip of the tea. My mind was still a jumble. I'd said "mother" meaning Brocca, but it was Macha, the Ancient One, I saw in my mind's eye. "Brocca, my mother, was a slave but she gained my father's permission to leave. That's why she joined them, for her freedom. I don't know how far her beliefs run."

"If your mother was a slave, how did you get to be a druid?"

"I'm not a druid yet, not officially. I'm in training. My father is a druid but he, and our chief druid, threatened me with slavery. That's why I'm here."

"To spend time with a slave?" He smiled a little; he used the end of his shepherd's staff to push the embers in the fire. "Why would he threaten you?"

"All of this that we are doing. Dathi is right - there is power in the memories we have. A past before our past. The chief druid in my tuath wants that power."

"So you ran."

I drank more of the tea, listening to the soft bleat of the sheep.

"No one has offered to help me before," said Patrick. "No one has helped me to run away. Not Dathi, except for the baskets of food."

"He's set on his mission."

"Which is us?"

"He's told you about past lives? He mentioned it's not something you believe but everything that has happened to me motivated by it. It's the vision I see. I'm seeing it now. It is this but different. Another time. This pasture, the sheep, you here." And me with him but I couldn't explain it yet. I couldn't explain it to myself.

"Past lives are definitely not a Christian belief. Not at all. We die and go to heaven. Hopefully." He ran his hand over the knitted sleeve of the tunic. "This feels familiar," he admitted. "And I've never had clothing like this. I never met you until the Imbolc ceremony but you're familiar too."

He's understanding. I closed my eyes, hoping my thoughts reached Dathi. Dathi had been trying too hard to force a past that Patrick wasn't ready to see. It would come to him, and me, in time. I didn't want to interrupt the impressions he was having so I drank the tea in silence.

He stood to check the movement of the flock as the sun edged closer to the sea. "Are you going back to the village? It'll be dark before you return."

"I don't think I can walk back now. The memories..." I recalled Mother's warning again. The effects of the Test did weaken me, sicken me.

I closed my eyes and let another vision play out. It was like waves, one after the other. Maithghean shouldn't have wasted his time with the Test. If he wanted my memories, he should have brought me to this lonely shepherd...The images continued...a round house, inside, a trunk filled with a warrior's things, a shield, a heavy sword. I gasped - back to the present - with Patrick. The shield the sword, a battle, a loss-

"Brigid, stop it." He handed me bread and cheese. But I closed my eyes again. I had to follow the shield, stored away, hidden away, the sword. Patrick shook my arm and forced me back. "Enough! Don't let that vision take you down. You need your strength."

"Did you see it?" I asked. "Any of it?"

"Did I see anything? No. Just you ready to faint." He ate the bread in huge, hungry bites. "Once or twice, I thought I heard a voice here. A lot like yours." He grinned. "Don't tell Dathi."

"Dathi doesn't know?"

"He knows I've learned the language. I picked it up from the raiders fairly quickly."

Even though I knew he didn't learn an entire language in a day or two, I let it go. He'd resisted so much - who could blame him? And I had to rest.

"I'll set up the lean-to." He set in the stakes and pulled over the tarp with quick military efficiency. "Come on."

I nearly fell into the tent, exhausted. He wrapped my cloak and wool blanket around me. He stayed in front of the fire, his new wool covering wrapped around him.

"Patrick." It was dark. He must have fallen asleep before he could bank the fire. Rain pattered on the lean-to and had dampened the embers. I had quartz and flint with me but it was too wet to light a new fire outside. I rummaged in my basket at the entrance of the tent for a candle. "Patrick." I called his name again. I used the stones and sent the spark to the wick.

He sat up. "Brigid. Where are you?"

"Here. Come in out of the rain."

He crawled under the lean-to with his blanket. Water had beaded on his wool tunic but he wasn't soaked through. It was cramped - clearly his makeshift lean-to was for one - and I shook out my cloak and pulled his blanket over him as we lay down, candle at the head.

"I thought you'd gone," he said. "I was having some kind of dream where you had left, you were gone, back to-"

"I'm here now, Patrick."

"Why did you leave?" He spoke as if he experienced it as reality, not as a dream.

"I'm not sure. He took something from me, I think. He had something important but I haven't figured it out yet." The images flashed and my head spun again. I knew the myths, I knew the stories. But the truth of that wasn't something I could face. "I can't work with the past anymore tonight."

"Don't leave." He was still in his dream state, the dream was real to him. I blew out the candle and settled closer to him, my head on his shoulder. He turned and pulled me to him, and we slept curled together, two broken pieces that fit into place.

CHAPTER 33

Brigid

Patrick sat under an oak, eyes closed. I wouldn't keep questioning him, like Dathi did. Let the memories come to him. I sat quietly on his other side. He had dreams - he'd flail and talk in his sleep - but often failed to remember them in the morning. I decided to stay with him in the pasture for a few more days, certain Dathi would not mind. I had important work to do here; Dathi had insisted on it. If both of us could begin to remind people about the Danann, speak to them in conversation, not in druid talk, then maybe the war chieftains like Dunlang and war druids like Maithghean would lose their power. They'd stop manipulating people to gain land, they'd stop battles, they'd stop taking people as slaves.

I spoke softly as Patrick went deeper into his meditation. "Recall Macha and Dagda. They fought to save us from the Fomorians...in the end, we had to form an alliance. It was the only way to save the Danann." I repeated the story I'd been told since childhood but there was more to it. It was me. Brigid, the other Brigid. I had been part of that alliance in a marriage to Bres. I kept my breathing steady as I continued. I had to separate memory from emotion. As Patrick struggled to recall any parts of his past, I worked to overcome the physical effects and not let the memory weaken me again.

Snoring. I opened my eyes, and there was Patrick, leaned back against the oak, mouth open and snoring. By all the gods...!

"Patrick!"

He startled awake. "Sorry."

"How are we ever going to figure this out if you keep falling asleep?"

He stood, stretched, and surveyed the sheep. I had to admit, his dedication to the animals was steadfast. He was good with them, keeping an eye out for wolves and foxes, fixing injuries. "*You* want to figure this out. You and Dathi. Not *we*."

"But you're part of it. You know you are," I added when he started to shake his head.

"Whatever you say. Meditation doesn't work for me. Tell me a story, let me sleep and dream, anything but sitting still under a tree. Come on -" he grabbed my hand - "See that lamb there, past that outcrop? She's straying too far."

We broke up the camp and walked down the hillside, hand in hand. I don't know why I felt self-conscious about it. We slept curled together every night, like puppies. We fit together. But sleep was all and him taking my hand was different. I wondered if maybe his meditation had worked in some way, if he was remembering the past life that was his.

He found the stray lamb and carried it to the flock. "Sheep don't see well," he explained. "They are just sort of slow and low to the ground. It's hard for them to know if a predator is near or they are at a cliff, until it's too late." We surveyed the flock and Patrick reached for my hand again. I felt a flutter at my center. Not a memory. Something present. Now. Our eyes met. We both blushed. This is ridiculous, I thought. We've been together for days, sharing the lean-to. We walked quietly, circling the flock. Patrick stopped and pointed out a limping ewe. "Your turn," he said and handed me a knife from his satchel. "I usually trim their hooves at the farm, and before shearing, but they seem to need it more this year."

He walked slowly toward the animal, careful not to startle the others. He grabbed her, and pushed her to her side. She bleated and the rest of the flock backed away. I kneeled on her side and inspected her hooves while Patrick sat on his heels, smiling.

It had been a long time since I'd done this chore, my more recent years taken up with druid training. I missed it, working with the animals.

"You're good at this," he said.

"I took care of my own flock for a while, before I began the druid path."

We let the ewe go on her way and grabbed for the next. "Tell me about Fothar-it."

"It's on the other side of the island, near the water where the sun rises. Even though my father was a druid, we had a farm. Mostly for my mother because she had a way with animals."

"I thought she was a slave."

"She was, but there are ranks of servitude." I said no more, not wanting to tell him that he was one of the lowest ranked servants.

You're enjoying this, aren't you? Having someone else do your job." I grabbed the next ewe and inspected her front hoof.

"You're just earning your stay, Brigid, in my luxurious home." He motioned to the tent on the hillside. "My real home was actually luxurious. A villa, with a beautiful courtyard. Fountains. Flowers. There's so much I took for granted.We even had servants but we treated them much better. Siculus was like family."

I trimmed off the excess growth on the outside and back of a ewe's hoof, and then checked the inside. This was the delicate part. I completed the task and let the ewe up. "There. Done." I turned to Patrick, beaming. I was proud of myself.

"Tell me more about your past in Fotharit. This past...not the one Dathi is trying to get you to remember. How were you raised as a druid's daughter?"

I told him about Mother and Alba and her life with Father. I told him about Maithghean and his lifetime of questioning me. "When I had a vision at Druin Criadh, that's when I understood there was something truly different about me."

"And you saved your chieftain?"

He seemed particularly interested in the battle and I had explained how combat of champions was usually a first choice. We discussed the two sides meeting on the field, the armor, the swords and shields. Patrick was particularly in awe of the custom of keeping a trophy head. "The Romans have done it in the past, I suppose. They're no stranger to blood. But a house? A trophy house?"

I finished the ewe I'd been working on. "Done."

"Good. Tomorrow we have ninety-nine more to go."

"Tomorrow." I handed the blade back to him and flexed my hands. Trimming was hard work.

We brought the tools up to camp when we found Dathi waiting for us on the boulder. His druid robes flapped in the breeze that came off the ocean and the sun shone brightly on his bald druid tonsure.

"How is the training?" He asked, friendly as usual. I didn't want to tell him that our conversations had turned to our most recent pasts, our current lives, not the ancient ones. Patrick walked past and sat at our fire pit, He rummaged through the basket Dathi had brought. Bread. Cheese. No venison.

"I'm remembering a lot," I said. "Too much."

"It's making her sick," said Patrick. He ran the trimming blade over a stone. Dathi inclined his head toward Patrick and I nodded. The memories were coming faster because of him. "Patrick is dreaming more, but he doesn't remember his dreams in the morning."

Patrick whisked the blade across the stone, louder. "I think we both need a plan, Dathi. A tangible plan. We can try for our memories, or for me, gain them, and then what?"

Dathi joined us around the fire I'd started while Patrick continued to sharpen the blade. "And then we travel. We visit tuaths across the land. We speak of the Old Ones. We bring them back to people's consciousness. For the druids, we introduce new rituals, or really, return to the old ceremonies, the ancient words. This is why for you, Brigid, being a druid of Foclut Forest or Fotharit is not enough. I envision you as Brigid of the Tuatha dé Danann, to be the druid of the entire land."

I was overwhelmed with what Dathi proposed. Before I could speak, Patrick threw down his blade and stone. "Sure Dathi. I'll travel along with you and the Druid of Éire over here. No worries. I'll run back here at night to check on the sheep. Clear away the foxes and wolves then meet up with you to tell stories around the fire. Great plan."

Dathi closed his eyes. "I'm working on procuring your freedom from Milliuc."

"I'll be free?"

"Not exactly." Dathi seemed to search for a way to explain. Freedom to servants could be granted with certain permissions. Children of a second generation could be freed. But none of these situations fit Patrick. Milliuc was a powerful landowner, second to the chieftain. He wasn't going to willingly let Patrick go. Servant exchanges must be of equal value based on the law, servants, and levels of freedom.

Dathi must have been in very delicate negotiations with Milliuc. "Unfortunately, you've done too good of a job, Patrick. Milliuc's flock has increased. There's more lambs, more wool for trade. He has little reason to grant your freedom or to trade you for someone else. So I am trying to compromise."

"Compromise?" asked Patrick. He picked up his tools and began scraping the knife against the stone loudly.

"I've offered to replace you with a new shepherd boy, at my own cost, and take you as my own. Milliuc would get double payment."

Patrick looked at me and then back to Dathi. "So I would be *your* slave? And some other boy would have to spend his life with Milliuc? So the three of us can travel around and *talk* to people?"

"Nothing is final yet," said Dathi. "And you would not be a slave to me. I would not treat you as one."

"But according to your Law?"

Dathi ignored his question and continued. "I had hoped you and Brigid would come to an understanding. You would remember your part in the past, as a founder of Éire and help cultivate the reverence for those who came before."

Patrick paced around the fire, fist clenched and face red. I'd never seen him this angry. "Have either of you considered that I want to go home? My home. Britannia. You want me to talk to people? I'd like to talk to my parents. I'd like to tell my mother and father that I'm alive. I hope to God *they* are alive."

Dathi bowed his head. He'd been so caught up in my Test of the Ancients and past memories, I was fairly certain he hadn't considered Patrick. "I see."

Patrick glowered at the both of us before he stalked downhill toward the stream. After a few moments, there was a glint of sunlight. He had caught a salmon.

"I don't understand," said Dathi. "I have seen it. Both of you, speaking before multitudes, bringing healing to the land."

"Maybe this will take more time, Dathi. Is there a way Patrick can go home? Even for a while? And how will I be protected? I cannot travel without the druid plaid." I had my own safety to consider.

"I'm working on that too. Raven and I both are. We're consulting with bards to find ancient ceremonies, something close to what the Danann would have used. She wants a plaid woven for you with all the colors of the land."

All the colors. Ancient ceremonies. A chill went through me. "Would other druids elsewhere accept that ceremony? Maithghean wouldn't accept it."

"They'd have to." Dathi departed, leaving us with a plan that I didn't know how to fulfill.

CHAPTER 34

Brigid

We journeyed with the flock through green pastures decorated with yellow and white daisies, outlined with patches of tiny red valerian flowers. Woodlands interrupted the landscape, and he camped under a thick forest of tall oak. We tended to the sheep and I told Patrick stories as we worked.

I told him of the Danann battles, Nuada, and the Lia Fail. Sometimes he'd interrupt and say Dathi had already told him. The story. Then I told him the story of Bres - he was intertwined with the rest. I spoke as a recitation, I told the story I knew. Brigid's marriage to Bres, how Bres tricked everyone to gain the kingship, the battles that divided our people. But it wasn't the story I *felt*, not the one I remembered as a part of my past.

"There's more to it," Patrick said. "You're leaving something out."

"Did Dathi already tell you this?" I ignored the glare of his blue eyes and touched the ewe with bilberry dye. We were in a far pasture that bordered another farmer's land. Patrick insisted we re-dye Milliuc's sheep to make sure they didn't get mixed in with another farm. I followed her quick exit to the pasture to find some of the younger animals. I was getting as good as Patrick in catching them and marking them with dye.

"Yes, to answer your question," he said. "Dathi told me the story of the final battles where the Danann defeated Bres."

"We all joined together, all the members of the tribe, even those who had been sent away." I looked at him pointedly to see if he recalled any of this.

"You weren't at the final battle," Patrick said. He reached for the dye pot and let the sheep go.

"How do you know I wasn't at the final battle?"

He started to answer and then paused, knowing he'd been caught. Finally he said, "I had a dream that I was looking for you. Searching. All I saw was stones on the beach. I wanted to kill the man who had caused a boy's death, but I couldn't. Not without you knowing, without your permission. It was your fight to end."

"You remember this?"

"It's a dream I've had, more than once. And what about you? You have nightmares. You wake up screaming and you terrify me."

I knew the story and I knew the truth. The loss. The images of the sword and shield came to me. And a boy, my boy, copper haired and smiling, taken by Bres, and killed in an assassination plot gone awry. That was the nightmare. The truth. The past. I'd wake with a start, sometimes a scream, and Patrick would hold me until I stopped shaking.

I let another sheep go and pointed to the mountain. "Let's camp up there for the night." I wanted to keep moving before more visions overtook me. From the mountain, I could point out the paths, the roads that led to his home.

The weather warmed and we kept the sheep nearer to streams and springs. Dathi hadn't returned and I worried about his negotiations. I wanted Patrick to be free from Milliuc. I wanted to be free from Maithghean. Somehow, we'd figure out a plan for Patrick to return home temporarily. That was the part I had yet to plan with Patrick; to convince him to return to   Éire. He was part of the Danann, part of the beginning. He needed to be here as much as I did.

Patrick set up camp and while I gazed upon numerous bonfires in the distance to the south. I should be with the druids now, performing the summer rites, the handfasting rites, the marriage rites.

"What's going on? Another pagan ceremony of some sort?"

"It's Beltane today," I said.

"What is it?" Patrick asked. "I see the fires from up here every summer. And I think there is a similar festival in Britannia. My friend Brawen..." His voice faltered.

"Go on." I took his hand in mine as we watched the celebrations below.

"I said something stupid once to a friend." He shook his head as if he wanted to forget.

"Beltane is the festival for summer, a time when marriages are created. There is much dancing, wreaths of daisies and red clover, joyfulness—a holiday of celebration." We heard faint chants of the people.

"I've always been in the pasture for this pagan festival."

"You keep using that word, *pagan*..." I said.

"I guess I do. Beltane is not Christian, that's for certain. People do all sorts of things."

"What sorts of things?" I elbowed him, hoping to lighten his mood. It was Beltane, after all. He gave me a sideways smile and blushed. "What do the Christians do this time of year?" I asked.

"Easter, I guess. We celebrate the resurrection of Christ. Flowers are everywhere there, too. My mother took pride in the daffodils in her garden."

"So it's a celebration of Resurrection? Rebirth?"

"Mostly it's about somber priests and sour communion wine." Faint drum beats echoed across the land, staccato, and reminded me of how isolated we were, how isolated Patrick had been for years."How do the memories work? How do you remember?"

"The memories are like all memories. Some are clear, some are farther away - think about something from your childhood. You recall the event but maybe not the details? And some are like dreams. Hazy. Impressions that don't always make sense."

"How did you come to marry Bres?" he asked suddenly. "Don't tell me a story like Dathi does. Tell me how you remember it."

I didn't want to talk about the past. Not tonight.

"Brigid, please. I've told you everything about me. You keep saying I'm connected to it."

Something in his voice prompted me. Again the familiarity that ran deeper than the few months I'd known him, here in the pasture. "After the first invasion, the Danann found that the only way to survive was to ally with the enemy. An alliance meant marriage. I - or Brigid of the Tuatha dé Danann- agreed to marry Bres of the Fomorians so the people would survive."

Patrick tensed and held my hand more tightly. "They purposely married you to the enemy, Bres, the man who nearly destroyed them all. Bres was your husband. Not me." Jealousy seemed to gnaw at him. "I should have been with you, not him. Wait, I can't - when was this? When did I know you? How?"

"Let the memories come. The more people remember, the stronger we all become. Even at that festival down there, no one is saying the name of Fodla of the streams. Warriors do not send their thoughts to Dagda before battles as they could. All of that power directed toward the Danann could help all of us."

"Dathi once said I had the makings of a druid. What do you think?"

I smiled. "It would help if you believed in some of this. And the druid path takes years. Most of us begin as children. But if you wanted to..." He shook his head so I continued on. "You can speak to the people. You don't have to be a druid. Conversations, stories, reminders. That's all. Please, *Padraic*. For us."

I'd said it. The Old Name.

"Your touch is something I know," he said quietly. "Your scent. Like clover. I can't explain it. It's familiar. You're familiar."

I held his hand tightly. He wanted to remember. He wanted, for the first time, to understand our connection.

"Whenever I feel ready to grasp it, my mind goes blank. Like waking from a dream. I know something was there but then it's gone."

A soft hoot of an owl filtered through the rustling breeze.

He continued. "Aren't you angry at the way they treated you? Forcing you into a marriage? Why revive these people? Or gods?"

"Patrick, marriages are arranged all the time. Look at your own family. Was everyone lucky enough to marry for love?"

"I guess it's different because I -" He stopped. "My parent's marriage was arranged. But my grandfather told stories of his parents, my great-grandparents. A forbidden marriage between a Christian man and pagan-raised woman."

"Carrying on the family tradition?" I leaned against him, hoping he would relax with the joke. He didn't. "A lifetime is short," I finally said. "What I bore with Bres was momentary."

Pensive, he asked, "What about love? What about Bres? Didn't you want him to care about you, at least a little? You deserve that much."

"I never expected it from him. Not from Bres." His questions were treading into areas I pushed from my thoughts. I wanted to keep the memories in the past and only access the Danann when needed.

But Patrick returned to what he knew and understood. Love. "I didn't ask if you expected it. I asked if you wanted it."

"I did want love, and found it, with someone else."

"Who?"

"You know the answer."

"Brigid, tell me. Please."

I sighed, giving in to weeks of frustration. "You remember none of it...*Padraic*...so it doesn't matter, does it?" My tone was bitter. I was tired of being the one who remembered everything. He resisted Dathi, he resisted me, and only wanted us to tell him without doing any of the work.

"Brigid, I want to remember." He let go of my hand, equally frustrated.

Patrick - wait.

He heard. He must have heard. I reached out to him as he stood. He pulled me up to him. Ran his fingers lightly over my hair, under my chin. Tilted my face to him. We kissed then, something hungry and new, something familiar. I couldn't let him go then and pulled him closer. For days now, weeks, I wanted this and so did he. He was tall and leaned down to me again, our kisses turned to heat. Done was the innocent hand holding. I pressed myself closer to him.

Don't stop.

Brigid, I want you.

I heard him. We had spoken without speaking. We sank to our knees by the fire, not letting go as we fumbled through my skirts, pushed aside his tunic. We were together and he was inside me and I had forgotten this body, this life, and gasped in surprise at the quick pain. He paused, realizing, but I pushed toward him. *Don't stop.* We held tightly together until he cried out, and we lay with our hands touching each other with tiny whispers.

CHAPTER 35

Brigid

Patrick and I woke before sunrise. A few of the Beltane fires still burned but mostly we saw the glow of embers. As I built our own fire for tea, a sense of unease filled me. Maybe it was the memories. I handed him his tea and settled in, my back against his chest, so that his arms and legs held me close.

"You heard me last night, silently, didn't you?"

"Maybe."

"Why don't you want to admit that the connection is there?"

"There is definitely a connection." He pulled me closer, if that were possible.

"You know what I mean."

We sipped on our tea avoiding the ever present conflict. Finally Patrick spoke. "I am angry, Brigid. I'm a slave. I've been here for years as a slave, forced to do Milliuc's bidding. Then you and Dathi come along and want me to share all these myths, these old stories that aren't even mine."

"But they are yours."

"Maybe they once were. I can even believe we were together in the past. But I am not that person anymore. I'm *not* Padraic of the Tuatha dé Danann. I am Patricius of Bannaven Taberniae. My grandfather is a deacon in the Christian church. I'm training in the Roman army. When I have served and have become an officer, I'll follow my father's career as a prefect. I'll collect the taxes for the town. This is who I am."

I had no answers except to wonder about the feasibility of Dathi's plan. I'd wanted to escape Maithghean and find safety wherever I could, so I agreed to it.

"And for harvest," Patrick said, "I will have to return to the farm. I will have to spend the winter with Milliuc. And where do you get to go? Inside the luxurious druid lodge?"

"No." I thought about it and took a deep breath. "You don't have to go back to Milliuc. Remember, I told you. I know the road that will lead you to the harbor. If you really want to go..." I took a deep breath because that was not what I wanted to say. "Promise me that you'll return. Keep to Dathi's plan."

"Come with me."

I hadn't thought of leaving, not really. Dathi and Raven had to help me complete my training or at least give some sort of ceremony. But to go to Britannia? To a Roman village?

"What if you stayed? Not here," I added when he shot me an incredulous look. "What if we went somewhere together, away from Milliuc and for me, away from Fotharit."

"I have to tell my parents I am alive. I have to see them."

Again, I closed my eyes, wishing I could ward myself from selfishness. I'd taken many things for granted - the fact he was here, not thinking about his kidnapping, or his family. "Of course. You have to see your family. We'll make our plan. Together. As soon as I am initiated as a druid, I can travel."

"Because you're not in any safer place than I am, are you?" He pulled the wool blanket around us both and held me tightly.

"Not really. I need the druid plaid for my freedom. Dathi said he and Raven had a plan. It could happen soon. Maybe at Lughnasadh."

"And then we'll go?"

"We'll go." I let the blankets drop and stood, facing the sunrise. "If we stand here at the top of the mountain, I can show you the roads east."

I walked alone through the forest, returning on the path Dathi had shown me a few months before. It was a quicker path than following the sheep trail over the rolling hills. I felt incomplete without Patrick, as if I were missing my cloak on a cold day. The warmth was gone.

We'll be together soon, I told myself. All I needed was the initiation ceremony. Or a druid plaid. I was willing to settle for just the cloak. Would I steal one? The thought crossed my mind. I wouldn't steal. Not really. I didn't need thievery as a reason to be caught either. I'd wait for a ceremony. Then Patrick and I would leave. We'd remain true to Dathi's mission and we'd add to it. We'd carry the Danann stories over the sea to the British tribes. They'd been defeated by Rome for centuries. They needed their ancient ones too. I'd meet with the tribes. Patrick said his friend, Brawen, followed the old ways. We could create a plan to revive *all* of the druid world.

That's how I would explain to Dathi where we were going and why. I tried to imagine how Patrick would fit in living in a druid house. None of it mattered. Patrick couldn't stay. He had to go home. He had to see his family.

Patrick had suggested we leave right then from the pasture.

"I can't abandon Dathi," I argued. "He needs to know we've left. And we need food, shelter."

"We've made do with the lean-to. I can catch fish. We've survived in the pasture, we can survive as we travel."

"I can't go without a druid title," I said. "Otherwise, any druid from Fotharit has the legal right to take me back there. I need that protection. "

He heard my words about slavery and the Law, but because I was raised as I was, and treated as a guest by Dathi, I don't think he understood truly about my slave status. Even so, he relented.

The path meandered through the forest and led to the ring fort.

There, at the gates, were the druids of Fotharit. The Fotharit plaid with its stripe of bright yellow. Maithghean's cloak. And next to him, Elían. Her cloak contained the yellow and a thread of green, representing the healing plants, the color of my acolyte cloak lost in the fire. They were speaking with Dathi and Raven.

A cold terror washed over me. They'd found me. I never thought they would have traveled so far, that Maithghean would find me here, far to the west. Dathi's head lifted from their enclosed circle of conversation, as if he sensed my presence. Maithghean's did too. His yellow eyes searched for me.

I should have hid in the forest. I should have turned to stone. I should have reached for the untapped goddess powers that I barely understood. I stayed absolutely still.

"Brigid," called Maithghean. It was a gamble. He hadn't seen me. Yet. "We've been waiting for you."

My only thought was of Patrick, alone on the hill, waiting for my return.

CHAPTER 36

Patrick

Patrick threw himself into his shepherd's work. He checked the dye on his flock. He made sure the young lambs didn't stray from their ewe. In the evenings, he busied himself with building a fire to cook salmon he caught from the stream. He wrapped his wool cloak around him as the food cooked, longing for the sound of Brigid's voice.

It had been three days and she hadn't returned. Then four days. Then five. She'd said three. And if there was a delay with some druid thing she was trying to obtain, certainly Dathi would have sent word.

One week. Then two. The full moon waned to dark.

He returned to the booley hut and repaired an old fence to pen in the flock. He walked the path to the fort, searching. She wasn't there. No trace of her in the forest. The warriors stood outside the fort's gates. Patrick melted back into the forest. He thought about running into the village and begging Dathi for help. But the guards would bring him to Milliuc. They would beat him again. Send him to live in the lambing shed. Dathi could have found him if he chose. But Dathi did not visit. Patrick returned to the pasture.

His dreams, vivid with Brigid, began to wane with the moon. Every night, he saw her face and heard her voice. Now, nothing. By the month's end, he understood that she was gone. She had left. Perhaps she became the Druid of Éire and had no use for him. Perhaps she chose the druid's cloak over him.

Yet, he lay awake and reviewed his weeks with Brigid repeatedly in his mind. Her body had been real. He'd breathed in the scent that was uniquely hers, the earth and fresh clover. It was only then, when he was with her like this, that it all made any kind of sense. When they joined together, when she fit perfectly into his arms, he could stop his mind from spinning around the whole druid idea of past lives, histories built upon histories. They'd created their own fire, their hearts a drum beat of their own. He had tasted her salty tears at the corners of her eyes. He knew his flesh had merged with hers.

"Where are you?" Patrick asked bitterly, as he had so often since she left. At least through the winter months, he had dreams and visions to rely upon. Now, there was nothing. Maybe the entire spring had been a vision too. One of Dathi's druid spells. Or hallucinations. He'd been hit in the head enough times. Too many beatings made his brain go soft.

By midsummer, he realized it had all been a figment. The boys at the farm had warned him of the fairies. A fantasy. He wanted a woman, that was all. All young men dreamed of beautiful women. She'd been a na daoine sí to taunt him in the night.

Yet. Brigid had shown him the road. South. And then east.

He climbed the mountain and studied the pathways again.

He had a choice. He could return to the farm at harvest. Or.

One day, when the fog was thick, Patrick ran. All he knew was to run. The dense fog enveloped him, and craggy limestone shredded his poorly shod feet with sharp accuracy. He refused to stop, even though he had in his bag some sheepskin to wrap around his feet.

Dogs panted and growled from someplace behind him. The guards had spotted him when he missed the cattle road Brigid had shown him. He continued south to a strange stone-covered land that cut his leather slippers, and still, the warriors and their hounds followed. They were close. This spurred him on over the sharp expanse of moonscape.

Limestone gave way to spongy soil, and he thanked God for the cool relief on his bleeding heels. He pounded on, sure of his goal and filled with enough faith to believe he would make it.

He skidded on loose rock, falling face first. Wryly, he wondered if he should thank the Lord again. He reached to grasp onto something solid, but there was nothing. He clutched at a cloud, arms and torso dangling. He blinked again, disoriented by the fog. The moon shone through the low-lying haze, clearing a path for his vision.

Crashing waves hurtled themselves against jagged rocks. He fought to keep his precarious balance and gasped as moonlight bounced off the waves of the western sea, illuminating the crags and coves that awaited his fall.

He dug his bare toes into the moist soil, the only solid thing he could feel, struggling for any hold he could find. The hounds barked in the distance, and he nearly lost his tenuous grip. He ignored the quick drop in the pit of his stomach, held onto blades of grass with his toes, and inched back from the cliff's edge.

Shakily, he stood and stared at his bare feet, bloodied and beaten. He tied his pouch of belongings around his waist and left the strips of sheepskins tucked away. Had his thin slippers survived, he surely would have slid on the rocks and died. He turned, continuing south.

"Thank you, Lord, for giving me hope." He'd prayed on his final decision to try escape again. If he could get to the eastern harbor, he could hide on one of the Silure boats.

His blanket, water bag, and supply of dried meat in hand, he began to walk southward. He knew the land now. He knew how to climb trees to hide from the guards. He could tuck himself into spaces between boulders. He preferred the trees. More than once, he'd felt a sinking feeling when he scrambled between the rocks. He pushed off that sensation with a strong force of will and trained his mind on Britannia.

The harbor full of ships beckoned to him. Resolutely, he faced ahead, determined not to look back.

Goodbye, Brigid.

He was free. He ran.

Bibliography

B arry, Terry. *History of Settlement in Ireland.* London: Routledge, 1999.

Bitel, Lisa M. St. "Brigit of Ireland: From Virgin Saint to Fertility Goddess." Monastic Matrix. February 2001. http://monasticmatrix.osu.edu/comm entaria/st-brigit-ireland.

Bury, J.B. The Life of St. Patrick and His Place in History. London: Macmillian, 1905 (reprinted).

Cahill, Thomas. *How the Irish Saved Civilization.* New York: Doubleday, 1995.

Charles-Edwards, T.M. *Early Christian Ireland.* Cambridge: Cambridge University Press, 2000.

Condren, Mary. *The Serpent and the Goddess: Women, Religion and Power in Celtic Ireland.* New York: Harper Collins, 1989.

de Paor, Liam. *Saint Patrick's World.* Notre Dame: University of Notre Dame Press, 1993.

de Paor, Maire. Patrick: *The Pilgrim Apostle of Ireland.* New York: Harper Collins, 1998.

Ellis, Peter B. *Celtic Women: Women in Celtic Society and Literature.* Grand Rapids: William B. Eerdmans Publishing Company, 1995.

Ellis, Peter B. *Druids.* Grand Rapids: William B. Eerdmans Publishing Company, 1994.

Flanagan, Laurence, (Compiled by). *Irish Women's Letters.* New York: St. Martin's Press, 1997.

Freeman, Philip. *St. Patrick of Ireland.* New York: Simon and Schuster, 2004.

Freeman, Philip. *War, Women and Druids.* Austin: University of Texas Press, 2002.

Gallico, Paul. *The Steadfast Man: A Life of St. Patrick*. London: Michael Joseph, 1958.

Greenhill, Basil. *The Archaeology of Boats and Ships*. London: Conway Maritime Press, 1995.

Gregory, Lady Isabella Augusta. *Irish Myths and Legends*. London: Running Press, 1998. (reprinted from 1910, John Murray, publisher)

Matthews, Caitlin, and John. *Encyclopedia of Celtic Wisdom*. Shaftesbury: Element Books Ltd, 1994.

McDonald, Theresa. *Achill Island: Archaeology, History and Folklore*. Tullamore: I.A.S. Publications, 1997.

McColman, Carl. "Is Brigid a Pagan Goddess or a Christian Saint? Yes." Retrieved from: www.beliefnet.com 7/29/2005, First published in Atlanta Celtic Quarterly.

MacCana Proinsias. *Celtic Mythology: Library of the World's Myths and Legends*. New York: Peter Bedrick Books, 1985.

MacManus, Seamus. *The Story of the Irish Race*. New York: Random House, 1921 original – 1990 revised edition.

McCone, Kim. "Brigit in the Seventh Century: A Saint With Three Lives?" *Peritia* 1 (1982), 107-145.

Ó Cróinín, Dáibhí. *Early Medieval Ireland*. London: Longman. 1995.

Ranelagh, John O'Beirne. *A Short History of Ireland*. Cambridge: Cambridge University Press, 1994.

Simmons, Paula and Ekarius, Carol. *Storey's Guide to Raising Sheep*. Pownal: Storey Books, 2000.

Squire, Charles. *Celtic Myths and Legends*. Bath: Parragon, 2003.

Starhawk. *The Spiral Dance: A Rebirth of the Ancient Religion of the Great Goddess*. San Francisco: Harper and Row, 1989.

Stokes, Whitley (trans) and Murphy, Ruth (compiled). "On the Life of St. Brigit." www.ucc.ie/celt: Corpus of Electronic Texts, CELT online at University College, Cork, Ireland. Text ID Number: T201010.

About the Author

Sheila R. Lamb's short stories are published in a variety of literary journals and she's been a writer-in-residence at Weymouth Center for the Arts and Humanities, a fellow at the Virginia Center for the Creative Arts (VCCA), and a contributor at Sewanee Writers' Conference. She has a long-standing fascination with Irish history and participated in Achill Island Archaeology Field School in County Mayo. During the day, she teaches history in the mountains of Virginia. She is the author of *Once a Goddess*. *Fiery Arrow* is the second book in the Brigid of Ireland trilogy. Follow Sheila on social media @sheilarlamb and on her website at sheilarlamb.com.

Photo © Shannon Hibberd

www.ingramcontent.com/pod-product-compliance
Lightning Source LLC
Chambersburg PA
CBHW020009140726
47904CB00018B/2140